CHRISTMAS MIRACLE PETS

Animals Who Saved the Day

Allan Zullo

SCHOLASTIC INC.

To Josie and Lucinda Rodell,
may the holidays and pets always make their lives
a little bit more magical.
— A.Z.

ISBN 978-0-545-38573-2

12 11 10 9 8 7 6 5 4   14 15 16 17/0

Printed in the U.S.A.   40
First Scholastic printing, November 2012

CONTENTS

 **Author's Note**

Whether you celebrate Christmas, Hanukkah, or Kwanzaa, the holidays are always a joyous time for the whole family. The season is a whirlwind of visiting friends and relatives, preparing delicious foods, exchanging gifts, and joining loved ones in traditions that have been passed down from generation to generation.

But kids and grown-ups aren't the only ones who make holiday memories. Pets do, too. Let's face it — most of us consider our pets members of the family. We include news about them in holiday cards and even buy gifts for them.

These loving creatures help make the holiday season special. In fact, I wrote a book about this theme called *The Dog Who Saved Christmas and Other True Animal Tales*, which was first published in 2008. Now I've gathered a new collection of stories about dogs, cats, birds, a goat, a rabbit, and a pig that turned the holidays into an unforgettable season. Each story is based on, or inspired by, a true-life event, but has been dramatized with re-created dialogue and scenes. In most cases, the names and places have been changed.

Some of the accounts in this book spotlight the mischievous side of family pets. Other stories feature heartwarming moments that illustrate the animals' loving natures. And many of these tales reveal how these remarkable creatures can teach us all about the true meanings of the holidays.

— A.Z.

The Dog Who Rescued Santa

Jack Mayberry made sure his snow-white beard and hair were curled just right. He tweaked his bushy eyebrows and mustache and adjusted his wire-rim glasses. After wriggling into a heavily padded, eight-pound, silk-lined red suit, he donned black boots and plopped a red cap on his head. Checking to make sure his breath was fresh, he took one last look in the mirror. Yep. He was ready.

Opening the door between the shopping mall's toy store and the upscale dress shop, Jack stepped into the main concourse, which was bustling with holiday shoppers carrying bags, pushing strollers, and scanning store flyers. "Ho! Ho! Ho!" he called with a hearty laugh that rumbled from deep inside his belly. "Good morning, everyone!"

"It's Santa! It's Santa!" little children squealed as they followed him down the concourse. And so began another day for the 67-year-old former international aid worker, who was beginning his eighth year as the Ledgestone Mall's jolly Santa Claus. When Jack reached the specially constructed "Santa Station" in the center of the mall, he sat in a large velvet chair where, for the next 11 hours (with breaks for lunch and dinner), he brought joy to hundreds of children and listened to their Christmas wish lists. He loved every minute of it. "I was born to be Santa," he used to tell his friends.

The best part was that his wife, Jill, had always shared the wonderful experience with him, playing the role of Mrs. Claus. She possessed a remarkable knack for calming wailing toddlers and babies who were scared about getting up close with the unusual-looking man in red.

But this year, Santa didn't have Mrs. Claus by his side. Two elves, played by college girls, assisted him instead. Jill remained at home, recovering from her second heart attack in ten months. Although she was starting to feel better, there was no way she could handle the long days at the mall as Mrs. Claus.

The couple loved kids but weren't able to have any of their own. Maybe it was for the best. Ever since Jack and Jill married right out of high school, they had dedicated their lives to helping children overcome hunger and disease in troubled spots throughout the world. Working side by side, the Mayberrys organized supply convoys in the war-torn Middle East, built clinics in India, dug wells in Africa, and taught school in Central America. It was the perfect job for them because they had no family. Each was an only child raised by a single parent.

After 40 years of global relief work, the Mayberrys returned to their roots in Massachusetts. Unable to afford a house, they rented a modest apartment near the food bank where they worked part-time.

During their first visit to the Ledgestone Mall, shortly before Thanksgiving, the Mayberrys noticed children staring and pointing at them and whispering things to their moms and dads. Finally, one brave five-year-old boy walked up to the couple and asked, "Are you Santa and Mrs. Claus?"

It was easy to understand why children would think the Mayberrys were Mr. and Mrs. Claus. Both were plump, wore glasses, and had rosy cheeks. Jill's gray hair was permed in tight curls. Jack sported long, wavy white hair that ringed his bald crown and matched his thick mustache and beard.

"Are you Santa and Mrs. Claus?" the boy repeated.

Jack laughed and replied, "No, young man. I'm one of Santa's cousins, and my wife is Mrs. Claus's sister." Bending over so he was eye level with the boy, Jack asked, "What's your name?"

"Adam."

"Have you been a good boy this year, Adam?"

"Yes, sir."

"Well, then. The next time I talk to Santa, I'll put in a good word for you."

By now a small crowd of children and their parents had gathered around the couple, asking questions about Santa and Mrs. Claus. Having dealt with children their whole adult lives, Jack and Jill enthralled the mall kids with stories about the North Pole, the elves, and reindeer.

When the group broke up, the Mayberrys began walking to the food court when they were stopped by Mr. Crabtree, the mall's director of operations, who invited them for coffee in his office. He told them he saw how they had interacted with the kids. Would the couple consider being the mall's Mr. and Mrs. Claus next year? Would they go to a Santa school for training first? Would Jack groom his white beard, and would Jill keep her gray hair permed? "Yes, yes, and yes," they answered. And so that's how Jack and Jill became the Ledgestone's Santa and Mrs. Claus.

But without Jill, this eighth year felt different for Jack. Oh, he still possessed that special twinkle in his eye, jolly laugh, and cheerful charm. But during those brief moments when he waited for the next child to climb into his lap, he thought about Jill. Every day she told him not to worry, that she was feeling dandy. Besides, she reminded him, the surgeon said the heart operation couldn't have gone any better.

Today was no different than the others for Santa. Jack held babies who were sleeping, wailing, or smiling. He beckoned to naughty kids, reluctant kids, and happy kids.

He posed for photos with toddlers, teenagers, and moms. And Jack ho-ho-ho'ed because he genuinely had fun.

However, by the end of the day, he was weary and achy — and anxious to get home to Jill. She always perked up when he told her the day's more unusual requests: today it was the girl who wanted a rainbow, the boy who asked for a live pet dragon, and the boy who begged to go to the moon.

"Did Sierra show up?" Jill asked.

"Yes. But she still isn't ready to sit in my lap."

Sierra was an adorable three-year-old who balked at meeting Santa. In fact, she was so frightened of him that she wouldn't even look in his direction the first time she saw him. Jack told her mom, "Don't force her. I'm sure you've been wisely telling her to beware of strangers, and now here I am — this fat, bearded guy in red. No wonder she's scared." The mother said, "I want her to overcome her fear — and I want a photo of her with Santa." So the mom had been bringing Sierra back to the mall daily for a week. Each time the little girl took a few steps closer to Santa before she would run back to Mommy.

"Be patient, because that little girl will soon crawl into your lap on her own," Jill told Jack. "Mark my words."

And so it went, 300 kids per day, seven days a week, from the day after Thanksgiving to Christmas Eve. And just as Jill had predicted, Sierra overcame her fear. "It took her ten days, but she finally climbed up on my knee all by herself," Jack announced to Jill shortly before Christmas. "The photo of her with me was perfect."

Jill clapped her hands in glee. "How wonderful! I wish I could have been there."

"Next year, Jill. Next year we'll be Santa and Mrs. Claus once again."

❄ ❄ ❄

Jack stood over the snow-covered grave of his beloved wife, not willing to believe she was gone, not willing to accept that her heart had failed. Hadn't the surgeon claimed the operation was a success? Hadn't he said she could resume a normal life by the end of January?

Yet here was Jack just a few days into the new year, shrouded in grief, alone in the cemetery. He was so numb he couldn't feel the wind-whipped cold even though his coat was unbuttoned. *We were made for each other — Jack and Jill — just like the nursery rhyme. Together . . . forever. What will I do without her? How will I go on?*

Jack had never lived alone before. Ever. As he realized the full magnitude of her death, he despaired. Weeping off and on, he tried to will his heart to stop beating. He took a leave of absence from his job at the food bank and shut himself off from the outside world. He declined all invitations from friends, stopped answering the phone, and seldom read his mail. The only time he ventured outside was to walk to the grocery store down the block for some frozen dinners, not that he had much of an appetite.

He spiraled into a depression so deep that he could barely function. Neglecting his hygiene, Jack went days between showers. He let his hair grow wild. His untidy beard and mustache took on a yellow cast from smoking cigarettes — a dangerous habit he resumed after decades of being smoke-free.

The apartment was neglected. No dusting, no vacuuming. He kept the curtains closed because the sunshine reminded him of happy and hopeful times — two emotions he just couldn't feel anymore.

Because he wanted to be left alone, he had few visitors. But one who checked on him every few weeks was Mr. Crabtree. He would bring Jack a bag of hot cinnamon buns from the mall. On one visit, he told Jack, "Jill would want you to go on living life to the fullest."

"Jill was my life," muttered Jack. "Now I'm nothing without her."

"Given the pain you've experienced from your loss, life will never be the same. But you have so much to offer. You're still our Santa Claus."

"No," Jack declared. "I will never put on that suit again. Find another Santa."

When spring approached, Jack was still depressed. But with money running out and overdue bills to pay, he returned to his part-time job at the food bank. His coworkers could see he was a shell of his former self. He wouldn't look anyone in the eye, talked little, and seldom smiled.

Learning that Jack needed more income to survive, Mr. Crabtree got him a job on the night-shift cleaning crew that worked from midnight to six A.M. at the mall. That was a perfect fit for Jack because it meant he didn't have to interact much with people — he talked little to the caring people at the food bank — which made it easier for him to wallow in misery. But that would soon change.

One day in September, Jack heard a soft bumping sound at his front door. He peered out the window but didn't see anyone. *Probably those kids in Building 3*, he thought. Then he heard it again. Grumbling, he cracked open the door. On his doorstep sat a medium-sized brown and white mongrel, wagging her tail and looking up at Jack. Her head and ears were the color of cinnamon, and she had a broad white streak from her nose to her forehead. The rest of her body was mostly white with large brown splotches. But the white in her matted coat was gray from grime. *Just some dirty, smelly mutt*, Jack thought. "Get out of here! Shoo! Shoo!" He slammed the door shut.

That evening when Jack was walking to his car to go to work, he was startled by the same dog as she scooted out from underneath his vehicle. *Dumb mutt.* When Jack came home shortly before dawn, he spotted the dog curled up under the bushes in front of his apartment. Seeing Jack, she bounded over to him, tail wagging, and circled him. Jack ignored her. The next night, as Jack got into his car, the dog bolted out from under the vehicle again. *Of all the cars in the parking lot, why is that mutt sleeping under mine?*

Returning home from his shift, Jack pulled into the parking space in front of his unit. The dog was waiting for him. For no reason at all, she seemed thrilled and excited to see him. But like the day before, Jack paid no attention to her.

The scene repeated itself for several days and nights. Because the dog had no collar, Jack assumed she was a stray. Still, he refused to pet her or say a kind word to her. *No dog should be that happy, especially a homeless one.*

When Jack came home from work about a week after the dog first appeared, he noticed that Doris Hartigan was picking up a bowl from the front step of her garden apartment next door. She was always so cheery, which he used to find delightful but now found annoying. *How could she be so merry? She's been a widow for years.*

"Oh, hello, Jack!" she said, waving.

He grudgingly nodded to her as the dog bolted over to him with another joyful greeting. "She's taken a shine to you," Doris said.

"Yeah," he acknowledged, not making eye contact with her or the dog.

"I know I shouldn't be feeding her because she's a stray, but I'm an animal lover, and I feel sorry for her," Doris said. "I don't dare call animal control because they'll put her to sleep."

"Uh-huh," said Jack, entering the house. *So that's why the mangy mutt is still around. She should sleep under Doris's car at night and deliver fleas to* her *doorstep. Whatever, I don't really care.*

But he was only kidding himself. The truth was he *did* care. In fact, he looked forward to being greeted by the stray. He even started petting her, and she responded by jumping up and licking his face. For the first time since Jill's death, his heart began to thaw.

"We really should do something about the dog," Doris told him.

"*We?*"

"Yes. Isn't it obvious that she's attached to you? She needs a home, and you need a companion."

"No, no," said Jack. "I've never owned a pet."

"Well, maybe it's time you had one. She'll give you unconditional love as well as be someone for you to love."

"Why don't *you* keep her?" he said.

"Allergies."

"I'm not ready for that responsibility."

"Well, then, let's look after her until I find a home for her."

Later that day, Jack went to the grocery store and found himself walking down the pet supply aisle. He hesitated. *I don't believe I'm doing this.* He placed a bottle of anti-flea-and-tick shampoo, a box of dog biscuits, and a bag of dry food into his cart. When he returned home, the dog was waiting for him. Jack picked her up — and got his cheek wet from her tongue. He put her in the tub and gave her a thorough bath that washed off dozens of fleas and ticks. Surprisingly, the dog remained calm.

After drying her off, he planned to put her outside. But it was raining, so he told her, "Okay, you can stay — but only for a little while." He poured some dry dog food in a bowl and set it down on the kitchen floor. Then he went into the living room and turned on the TV to watch the New England Patriots, one of the few pleasures he allowed himself. When she finished eating, the dog went over to Jack's chair and laid her head in his lap. He stroked her and soon felt a warmth inside him that he hadn't experienced in eight months.

When the rain stopped, he let her outside. After work, he stopped in a 24-hour Walmart and bought a leash and collar. Even though it was still dark when he returned home, he put the collar on the dog and took her for a walk. Over the next four days, they went on several walks. She was incredibly obedient and heeled close to his side. She knew basic commands like sit, stay, and come — and, best of all, she was housebroken.

On his walks, Jack's senses seemed sharper. He took notice of the crisp air tingling his nose, the leaves turning into a tapestry of autumn colors, and the wisps of smoke wafting from chimneys. With the dog merrily prancing beside him, his attitude seemed to brighten. He started talking more to his fellow workers, even cracking a few jokes. It felt good.

Doris knocked on his door. "Good news, Jack. I've found a home for the dog — a sweet, young family with two children. They'll be here this afternoon to pick her up."

He thought about saying, "No, I'll keep the dog." But he didn't. "Why, that's great," he replied halfheartedly. "The mutt will be much better off in a stable home instead of being left outside, what with me working two jobs. A good dog like her shouldn't be around an old depressed man like me."

When the family arrived, the kids — a boy and a girl in middle school — fell in love with the dog. She romped with them, rolled in the ground with them, and licked their faces. It looked like a good match. Jack gave them the dog food, biscuits, shampoo, and leash that he had bought. But when they led her to their car, she balked and whimpered.

With her tail curved between her legs and her ears drooped, she tugged against her leash.

"She's probably scared of cars," Jack explained. He picked her up and put her in the back of their vehicle. He petted her one last time and said, "Be a good girl, now."

She stared at him with sad puppy-dog eyes. Jack turned and walked into his apartment. He didn't want anyone to see his misty eyes.

After they drove off, Jack smoked more cigarettes. That evening he went to work at the mall feeling down. Just when he thought that he was beginning to climb his way out of his depression, he felt himself slipping backward.

At the end of his cleaning shift, Jack was getting into his car when Mr. Crabtree showed up and said, "Jack, one last chance. Will you be Santa again this year?"

Jack shook his head. "I can't. I won't. Get someone else."

Five days later, there was a knock on the door. When Jack opened it, he was caught off guard. There was the dog, jumping and pawing at Jack's belly. "You're back!"

Behind the dog was the man whose family had adopted her. "We can't keep her any longer," the man said bluntly. "We were led to believe she was well-mannered."

"She is," Jack insisted.

"No, she isn't. Ever since we brought her home, she's been misbehaving. She's growled at my kids, chased our cat, snapped at me and my wife, and refused to obey our commands. We were told she was housebroken, but she has soiled our carpet many times."

"I don't understand," said Jack. "She's been nothing but an angel with me."

"Good. Because she's yours again." He thrust her leash in Jack's hand, spun on his heels, and left.

Jack dropped to his knees and gushed, "Welcome home, girl!" He gave her a big hug.

Seeing Jack in his open doorway with the dog, Doris walked over to find out what had happened. After he explained, Doris said, "Humans don't always get to pick their pets, you know. Sometimes animals choose their humans. They just know. Jack, this dog picked you. I suggest you find a good name for her."

"I'm going to take my time, because I want to pick out the name that suits her best."

Jack felt happy now that the dog was back. He hadn't realized how much he had missed her. "I guess it's just you and me, girl. Well, if I'm going to care for you, I'd better care for me."

He threw away his cigarettes. He began eating healthier and taking longer walks with the dog. He had his hair, mustache, and beard shampooed and trimmed by a stylist. He spit-shined his apartment. "The time for self-pity is over, girl," Jack declared.

But it was easier said than done. He still missed Jill terribly and suffered occasional pangs of grief that triggered a crying jag. Whenever Jack hit one of those low points, the dog instinctively knew to rest her head on his lap, providing him with much needed comfort.

Overall, Jack was feeling better and getting stronger. *One step at a time*, he thought. *One step at a time.* And then it came to him: *Of course! I know what I'm going to call her.* Remembering the little girl who had taken a few steps closer each day for ten days before she would sit in Santa's lap, Jack held the dog's face in his hands and announced, "From now on, you're Sierra."

The dog gave a woof and wagged her tail as if to say she liked the name.

Joy was returning to Jack's heart. He began reconnecting with friends and showing off his cherished pet. He even brought Sierra with him to the food bank and on his late-night shift at the mall.

On Thanksgiving Day, Sierra accompanied Jack to a soup kitchen where he helped serve food to the homeless and needy families. The dog was an instant hit with the children, who petted and hugged her.

During a break, Jack went to each table to chat with the guests. At one table, a six-year-old boy named Cody asked, "Are you Santa Claus?"

"No, I'm not," Jack replied with a chuckle. "But I am

one of his cousins. Is there something you would like for Christmas?"

Cody pointed to his tattered, worn-out basketball shoes and said, "Yes, sir. A pair of sneakers that fit."

"I'll be sure to tell Santa."

"We don't have a home. How will he know where we live?"

"Santa has his ways."

While Sierra grabbed Cody's attention, Jack found out from the mother the boy's shoe size and the address of the shelter where they were staying. The next day Jack bought the sneakers, had them gift-wrapped, and left them at the shelter with a note from Santa, saying he wanted Cody to have an early Christmas present.

After eight holiday seasons, it felt weird not wearing his Santa outfit and sitting in the big velvet chair in the center of the Ledgestone Mall. He almost wished he hadn't insisted that Mr. Crabtree find a new Santa. But at the time, and the way he felt then, Jack simply couldn't imagine that he would ever want to play St. Nick again.

About two weeks before Christmas, Mr. Crabtree showed up at the mall at the crack of dawn as Jack and Sierra were leaving. "Jack, I need your help big-time."

"What is it, Mr. Crabtree?"

"My mall Santa got into a serious car accident last night. He broke both his arms. Can you . . . will you . . . ?"

"Be Santa?" *Thank goodness I didn't throw out the Santa suit!* "Yes, yes! Absolutely I will!"

"Jack, you are a lifesaver!"

"No, Mr. Crabtree," replied Jack. Rubbing his hand gently over his dog's back, he said, "Sierra is the real lifesaver."

# Cat Angel

Goats, sheep, and llamas were there. So were parrots, cockatoos, and parakeets. And horses, ponies, and donkeys. And dogs and cats, of course. Hundreds of them, many in tutus, doll clothes, and bunny ears or little pet T-shirts that read HOT DOG or I'M THE CAT'S MEOW or MAMA'S BOY.

Carrie Pritchard loved mingling with the animals. As the 12-year-old daughter of an Episcopalian priest, Carrie attended many religious ceremonies, but none was more enjoyable than this one — the Interfaith Blessing of the Animals. Every year in early October at various churches and parks throughout the world, animal lovers bring their beloved pets for a special blessing by clergy. The annual ceremony is held in honor of Saint Francis of Assisi, the patron saint of animals and the environment, who was known for his compassion for all living things.

Carrie and her brother, Cameron, 14, were animal lovers, just like their mother, Susan, and their dad, Mark, a priest at St. Luke's Episcopal Church, who was one of the eight clergy of different faiths taking part in this year's blessing at the local park. The Pritchards brought their two aging golden retrievers, Jimbo and Sambo, who liked meeting most of the hundreds of animals that were brought to the ceremony. All owners had to carry their pets or keep them on a leash, which was a good rule. The previous year, Jimbo tried to take a chunk out of the front leg of a grouchy alpaca that spit on him for getting too close.

Carrie was awed by the array of animals. Especially impressive were the 20-pound python draped around the shoulders of its owner and the baby kangaroo (a joey) in the strong arms of its handler. She petted a de-skunked skunk, a pair of large floppy-eared rabbits, a multicolored iguana, and two playful ferrets.

At the start of the ceremony, held on a mild Southern California day, Father Mark gave a short opening prayer to the crowd: "Dear Lord, we thank you for creating all the animals that inhabit the skies, the earth, and the sea. They share in the fortunes of human existence and play an important role in our lives. They are a reminder to us of the sanctity and variety of your creations. And because animals are not bound by any religious denomination, may we learn from their examples that peaceful coexistence can be a reality no matter the differences. We pray for the blessings of these beautiful creatures, and may we all treat them with the care and generosity that they deserve."

Nodding to his fellow clergy, Father Mark added, "And now let's confer God's blessing onto these marvelous animals." The eight clerics spread out over different sections of the park and began anointing the pets with holy water.

❄ ❄ ❄

Nine-year-old Hailey Wolcott had attended the ceremony the previous three years so her Siamese cat, Yada, could get blessed. But she didn't want to go this year, not when her heart still ached over that terrible day three months earlier. Hailey had taken Yada onto the front lawn even though she had been told never to let the cat outside for the pet's own safety. The girl kept her fingers wrapped around the cat's collar and was stroking Yada's head when suddenly . . . *KABOOM!* A fighter plane from the nearby naval airbase had triggered a thunderous sonic boom that rocked the neighborhood. People in the area were pretty much used to such booms, caused whenever a jet plane broke the sound barrier. Although the noise never bothered Hailey, it always sent Yada into a tizzy. Normally, she would scurry under Hailey's bed and hide there for several minutes before cautiously inching her way out.

But on that day, at that moment, there was no bed for Yada to hide under because she was outside in Hailey's lap. A split second after the sonic boom, the cat jerked and yelped. Hailey had a firm grip on her collar, but the feline was so terrified that she slipped out of her collar and darted off. "Yada! No! Come back! Come back!"

Yada could have run up the Bradford pear tree in the front yard or concealed herself in the thick lantana shrubs that separated the Wolcotts' yard from the neighbors. She could have zipped into the backyard and found any number of places to hide. Instead she shot willy-nilly toward the Yangs' house across the street. But Yada never made it to the other side. The driver of the flower delivery van did everything he could to avoid the cat. He slammed on his brakes and swerved to the curb, but it was all in vain.

Hailey was devastated. For days afterward, she blamed herself. *If only I hadn't brought her outside. If only I had held her tighter.* Her parents never faulted her, never lectured her. "Sometimes bad things happen that are beyond our control," her mom said.

Two months later, Hailey was on the floor in the family room, flipping through the TV channels. She stopped on Animal Planet, which was showing an injured cat being treated in a veterinarian's emergency room. Hailey grew teary-eyed and turned off the TV. She still missed Yada. She still missed how the cat would cuddle on her pillow at bedtime and play with her long raven hair and then, in the morning, gently paw her face to wake her up.

I want another cat, she thought. But it didn't look like that would happen anytime soon. She had approached her parents with the idea, and they said they would talk it over. That night she overheard them say that maybe when she was a little older, a little bit more responsible, she could have one. Okay, so maybe Hailey didn't always clean out the litter box as often as she should have and sometimes she failed to fill up Yada's dish in the morning, but that was only when the girl was running late for school (which happened a lot). Hailey thought she had done a fairly good job of caring for the cat.

"Maybe down the road we'll revisit your request," her dad told her.

She knew that was his way of saying no. *"Down the road" could mean, like, forever!* So Hailey decided to introduce a new, more responsible version of herself. Without being asked, she took out the garbage, kept her room tidy — well, at least she picked her clothes up off the floor; just don't look in her closet — and helped around the kitchen. She didn't mention a new cat. Not yet. The timing wasn't right. Late in September, a notice in St. Luke's church bulletin convinced her that now was the time to revisit her request. She would broach the subject in a clever and subtle way that, she hoped, would pull at her parents' heartstrings.

"Mom, Dad, would you take me to the blessing of the animals next week?" she asked.

"But, honey," said her mother, "we don't have any pets."

"Well, yes we do — sort of." Hailey held up her favorite stuffed animal, the Cheshire cat from *Alice's Adventures in Wonderland*. "I'll take Chessy to get blessed. It's the only cat I have." *When they see how sad it looks for me to bring my stuffed animal to the blessing, they'll* have *to get me a cat.*

So that's why Hailey was among all the pet owners and their animals at the ceremony. Now she was ready to spring the second part of her plan. After patiently waiting her turn in line, she finally reached Father Mark and held up her stuffed animal for a blessing.

"My, that's a big cat," the priest declared. Then he chortled. "Oh, it's not real."

Deliberately mustering up some tears, Hailey said, "My real cat, Yada, was run over a few months ago, so all I have is Chessy. I know it's not a live animal, but could you bless him, please, Father Mark?"

"Why, of course." In the same way he did for real animals and their owners, he sprinkled a few drops of holy water, placed his hand on the stuffed animal's head, and said, "Chessy, may you be blessed in the name of God, and may you and Hailey enjoy life together." Turning to her parents, he added, "I do believe that's the first time I've ever blessed a stuffed animal."

"Maybe next year I'll have a real cat that you can bless," Hailey said, flashing a yearning look at her parents. "Wouldn't that be nice?"

Father Mark nodded and turned his attention to the next person, a woman holding a Chihuahua decked out in a red tutu and matching bonnet.

Off to the side where they had just witnessed their father blessing Chessy, Carrie and Cam giggled. "Do you believe that?" Carrie whispered. "A stuffed animal? Really?"

"Dad looked like he wanted to burst out laughing," said Cam. "Who is she, anyway?"

"Hailey Wolcott. She's a fourth grader at St. Luke's."

❄ ❄ ❄

Early one evening a week before Christmas, Cam and Carrie were helping their mother carry packages from the car after a final round of holiday shopping. In the dusk, Christmas lights began to twinkle up and down the street. Suddenly, the Pritchard kids heard a scream coming from Mrs. Mangione next door. As Cam and Carrie rushed toward her, they saw a silver streak zoom in front of them.

"Mrs. Mangione, are you all right?" asked Cam.

Pointing to her ankle, which was bleeding, she grumbled, "It's that dang cat. I caught him digging up my zinnias, and when I tried to shoo him with my foot, he clawed me."

"Is that the silver tabby we've seen hanging around here?" asked Carrie.

"Yes. I don't know if he's a stray or he has been abandoned, but he's been a nuisance ever since he showed up last week. I'm not the only one who's been terrorized by him. Mr. Jenkins found him in his garage last week tearing up rolls of paper towels, and Mrs. Ruiz down the street said the cat was soiling her flower pots."

As they headed back to their house, Carrie told Cam, "We need to catch that cat before someone tries to harm him. He's a pretty cat and probably really scared."

"And what if we do catch him? Then what? He doesn't have a collar so there's no way to know who he belongs to."

"Maybe he has a microchip. We can't do nothing."

The next day, a Saturday, which was the first day of the long Christmas break, brother and sister hopped on their bikes and searched for the silver tabby. They stopped to question neighbors and learned that the cat had been spotted at the intersection of Cherry Street and Highview Avenue next to the estate of George Morton, a wealthy investor who valued his privacy, but was the town's biggest contributor to local charities.

Carrie and Cam pedaled toward the Morton residence, an estate that took up half a city block and was surrounded by a spiked iron fence fronted by a thick ten-foot-tall manzanita hedge. "Look!" shouted Carrie, pointing toward the hedge facing Cherry Street. "There's the cat!" Dropping their bikes across the street, they each put on a pair of their dad's work gloves and carried a canvas shopping bag, which they planned to use to carry the cat — if they could catch it.

Quietly, they crept up behind the silver tabby. But then he spotted them and disappeared into the hedge. They soon heard a long yowl. "It sounds like he's hurt or frightened," Carrie said. They crawled under the hedge, only to get smeared with mud because the dirt was soaked by the sprinkler system.

Despite the cold ooze seeping through their clothes, they kept searching in the hedge until they spotted the cat tangled up in the Christmas light cords that weaved through the branches. The cat was twisting and turning, trying to free himself.

"We've got to help him before he chokes to death," Carrie urged.

"You get on one side, and I'll get on the other and . . ."

Suddenly, they heard the *whoop, whoop* of a police car siren. "Police!" said a gruff voice. "Back out slowly on your stomachs and keep your hands away from your body."

"Oh, no!" gasped Carrie under her breath. "We're in big trouble."

"We didn't do anything wrong," Cam contended. "Just stay calm and do as he says."

They low-crawled backward from under the hedge and then rolled over to see two police officers, whose hands were poised on their gun holsters, standing over them. Next to the cops was the estate's caretaker. "Yep, those are the two sneaks I saw tryin' to break into the estate," he told the police.

"Why, they're just kids," the younger of the two officers said to his partner.

"What are you two doing here?" the older cop barked at them.

"We're trying to save a stray cat that's tangled up in Christmas lights, sir," Cam explained. Sensing that the cops didn't believe him, he said, "Go see for yourself. Maybe you can free him. The cat needs help. Honest."

The younger officer kneeled on one leg and peered into the hedge. "I don't see any cat in here," he said.

"I told you," said the caretaker. "These kids are up to no good."

"What are your names and where do you live?" the older cop asked them.

"I'm Cam Pritchard and this is my sister, Carrie. We live at Fifty-five . . . there it is!" Pointing to a silver tabby on the top of the hedge, he shouted, "That's the cat we're trying to save!" The animal had freed himself and struggled to make it to the corner of the estate where the hedge and iron fence met a thick, 12-foot-tall brick column.

From the corner column, the cat leaped out of sight into a large sycamore tree that had branches hanging over the

Highview Avenue side of the estate. While the cops, two kids, and caretaker were running to the corner, they heard the screeching of tires from a car. "Oh, no!" Carrie cried out. "The cat!"

After the five turned the corner and reached the sycamore, they saw nothing in the street except a convertible farther up Highview. There was no sign of the cat. They looked in the tree and searched a few nearby yards.

"The cat must have jumped to the ground and taken off," said the older cop. "It doesn't look like he was hit." Turning to Carrie and Cam, he said, "As for you two, I suggest you go home and clean up. And don't come snooping around here again."

"Yes, sir," said Cam. "Sorry, sir."

"If you spot the cat again, call animal control," said the younger cop. "It's their job to catch it, not yours."

Parroting her brother, Carrie replied, "Yes, sir. Sorry, sir."

❄ ❄ ❄

With their mother, Carrie and Cam stood beside their father in the church courtyard while he offered holiday wishes to parishioners following his Christmas Day service. Among those exchanging greetings were Hailey Wolcott and her parents.

"Merry Christmas, Hailey," said the priest.

"Prayer works, Father Mark!" she bubbled. "It really, really works!"

"I'm delighted you discovered that for yourself," said the priest. He looked quizzically at her parents for an explanation.

"Father Mark, you aren't going to believe what I'm about to tell you," said Mrs. Wolcott. "As you might remember, Hailey has been bugging us for months about getting another cat ever since her pet, Yada, was killed. Well, we kept putting her off, because we didn't really want another one. At night when she said her prayers, Hailey kept asking God to give us a change of heart so she could have a cat.

"I told her, 'If God gives you a cat, we'll let you keep it.' Well, last week, I was driving in our convertible with the top down, and Hailey was in the backseat and, this is what's so incredible. . . ."

"A cat came flying out of the sky and landed right in the car!" Hailey exclaimed.

Mrs. Wolcott continued. "It's true, Father Mark. For the life of me, I have no idea where the cat came from. He hit the inside of the door and was dazed, so I stopped the car and wrapped him in a blanket and went straight to the animal clinic. He stayed overnight and got checked out.

He was fine. The vet said that judging by the cat's teeth and the fact that he had been neutered, he had been someone's pet. But he had no collar or microchip so —"

Hailey interrupted, "Mom and Dad said I could keep him, and he's so sweet. I call him Angel."

Carrie and Cam stared at each other in astonishment. Then Cam asked Mrs. Wolcott, "Do you remember where and when this happened?"

"Certainly," she replied. "It was a week ago Saturday on Highview just past Cherry, right by the Morton estate."

"Was it a silver tabby?" he asked.

"Yes, but how would you know that?"

"It's a long story," he replied.

Shaking her head in wonder, Carrie added, "I guess you could say God works in mysterious ways."

The Christmas Pig

Tommy Segura pounded his fist on the steering wheel of his pickup and declared, "The Bears are going to annihilate the Packers. You can take that to the bank, bro."

"It's Green Bay all the way, baby!" countered his cousin Manny Colon, who was sitting shotgun. "Brett Favre and the Packers own the 1998 season."

Tommy, 17, and Manny, 16, were on their way back from visiting their grandparents, Tito and Tita, who lived in a small town near the Wisconsin–Illinois state line. The boys had just delivered several long tables and chairs for the big dinner that their grandparents would be hosting the following day, on Christmas, for 30 relatives.

Six inches of snow had fallen two days earlier, and although the country roads had been plowed, icy patches lurked on the pavement. That's why Tommy was driving slower than usual on the 15-mile ride back to the city.

"Let's bet on the game," Manny suggested.

"How much?" asked Tommy.

"Not for money. If the Packers win, you have to wear my Green Bay jersey to school the first day back from

Christmas break. If the Bears win, then I'll wear your Chicago jersey. Are you cool with that?"

Before Tommy could reply, a farm transport truck crammed with pigs lost control about 20 yards ahead of them in the same lane. The truck swerved violently to the left and then to the right before it straightened out. But unexpectedly something light brown and gray tumbled out of the back and onto the road.

"It's a baby pig!" Manny shouted.

Tommy slammed on the brakes and jerked the steering wheel to the right, trying to avoid hitting the animal. But his maneuver caused the pickup to spin in a full circle on a patch of ice while skidding forward.

"You're going to run over the pig!" Manny yelled.

The pickup slid directly over the animal and rammed into a snowbank on the shoulder. Fortunately, the boys weren't hurt because they were wearing their seat belts.

"Did you hit the pig?" Manny asked.

"I don't know. Everything happened so fast." They jumped out of the vehicle and looked behind them. Seeing the pig lying motionless in the middle of their lane, the boys warily walked toward him. "That's the biggest roadkill of my life," said Tommy.

When they reached the male piglet, Manny exclaimed, "He's alive! You went over him without hitting him." The animal — his body scraped up on his belly, chin, and back — was breathing heavily. "What should we do, Tommy?"

"We can't leave him here. There's a blanket behind the passenger seat. Go get it and put it on the pig. I'll run up the road behind us and warn any approaching cars to slow down and go to the other lane until we capture him."

By the time Manny returned with an orange and blue Chicago Bears blanket, the piglet had regained his senses and was on his feet. Seeing a human standing over him with a blanket, the piglet squealed and ran across the road and over the snowbank. "Yo, Tommy!" Manny shouted. "The pig took off! Now what should we do?"

"We have to go after him," Tommy replied, running back toward the pickup. "He's hurt and if we don't catch him, he'll freeze to death out here." He snatched the blanket from Manny. Then they chased after the frightened, injured animal, which kept changing directions in a bid to escape.

Holding the blanket in front of him, Tommy leaped toward the piglet, but the animal slipped out and Tommy ended up with a mouthful of snow. He brushed himself off and tried again. This time, Manny got in front of the piglet and slowed him down enough for Tommy to trap him under the blanket.

Once the piglet was secured and wrapped up, Tommy carried him back to the pickup. The animal expressed his displeasure by squealing and squirming. Inside the truck, Tommy handed the unhappy bundle to his cousin. "Merry Christmas, Manny."

"Hey, that's not funny. You take it."

"You're rejecting my Christmas present? Bad form."

"In case you forgot, I live in the city just like you. I can't have, nor do I want, a pet pig. Besides, this cute little guy is going to grow up to be an ugly big guy. So what are we going to do with him?"

"We could try to find an animal clinic, but who knows if any are open during the holidays. I think we should find him a home."

"Now, bro? Who's going to want a wounded pig on Christmas Eve?"

"Look around you. This is farm country. There must be a farmer who'll take him off our hands. Let's knock on some doors."

Fortunately, the pickup wasn't damaged, so Tommy backed out of the snowbank and drove to the nearest farm. When offered the piglet, the farmer there said, "I run a dairy farm. I have no need for a pig."

At the next house, a kindly farm woman examined the piglet's injuries. "Oh, you poor thing," she said in a baby voice. "You don't deserve to suffer like this. I can help you." Tommy and Manny were relieved — relieved, that is, until she told them, "If you want, I'll shoot it and put it out of its misery."

"That's not an option," Tommy declared.

Back in the truck with the piglet, Manny said, "Maybe you should reconsider. We won't find anyone who'll take him. All we're doing is prolonging the pig's suffering."

"There must be someone out here with the Christmas spirit willing to save a baby pig. Let's keep trying."

About a quarter mile away, they drove into a snow-packed gravel driveway that led to a yellow two-story gabled farmhouse. With the piglet wrapped in the Bears blanket, the cousins walked up the steps to the front door, which was adorned with a large Christmas wreath.

Holding the piglet — which had calmed down — with one arm, Tommy knocked. Answering the door was a tall girl about his age wearing an oversized University of Illinois sweatshirt. She was the prettiest girl Tommy had ever seen: a long blond ponytail, creamy skin, pink cheeks, and warm hazel eyes.

"Merry Christmas," she said, flashing a smile that revealed perfect white teeth. "Can I help you?"

Tommy was so taken by her beauty that he just stood and stared. Not until Manny jabbed him in the ribs did he stammer, "I . . . uh . . . I mean, we picked up this injured baby pig in the road . . . and, um, uh, he had fallen out of a truck in front of us . . . and, I, uh, I mean we were hoping we could find someone to take care of him." He unwrapped the blanket so the girl could see the animal.

"Oh my," she said, examining the piglet. "It looks like this little piggy has some serious road rash. Come on in. Let's see what we can do for him."

As she led them into the kitchen, she said, "I'm Kristin Jensen."

Because Tommy was instantly smitten, he stumbled over his words. "Hi. I'm Tommy, uh, Tommy Segura, and this is my friend, I mean cousin, Manny . . . uh . . ."

"Colon," said Manny, irked that his cousin was so tongue-tied that he momentarily forgot Manny's last name.

Kristin motioned for them to sit down at the table. She grabbed a washcloth, soaped it, and gently cleaned the piglet's wounds while Tommy held the whimpering animal. Then she reached into a drawer and pulled out an antibiotic ointment, which she put on the scrapes. Through it all, Kristin crooned sweetly to the piglet until he fell asleep in Tommy's arms.

"Wow, you have the magic touch," he told her.

"Oh, not really," Kristin replied. "I've just been around farm animals my whole life, so I've learned how to help them when they're hurt."

"What should we do with him?"

"Leave him with me. I'll take care of him. I'll raise him until he's really fat and then" — she slashed the air — "I'll butcher him!" Seeing the shocked look on the boys' faces, Kristin laughed. "I'm just kidding, guys. Don't worry. I'll find him a good home."

The three of them — well, mostly Kristin and Tommy — talked for the next hour about everything from school to music to football. Manny was the odd man out. Meanwhile, the piglet slept, interrupting the conversation with an occasional snort.

Finally, Manny said, "We better hit the road, Tommy. It's getting late."

Tommy could have stayed for hours, because he had never felt his heart stir like this over a girl. But it was time to leave. "Thanks, Kristin, for looking after the pig," he said as they walked out the door.

"And thank you both for caring enough to rescue him," she replied.

"Uh, do you think it would be all right if, um, you know, I gave you a call to, um, you know, check on the pig?" he asked.

"Sure," Kristin said. She went inside and returned, handing him a piece of notebook paper with her phone number written on it. Tommy noticed the penmanship was flawless.

On the ride back home, Manny said, "Man, you are gaga over that chick. It's a good thing you're buckled in, because otherwise you'd be floating on air."

Trying to hide his feelings, Tommy said, "She's all right."

"All right? Are you loco? She's beautiful and smart and funny. Man, what's not to like about her?"

"She's a Packers fan."

That night, all Tommy could think about was Kristin. He loved everything about her — the way her eyes danced, the way her ponytail swayed when she talked, the way she smiled. And her voice! To Tommy, it was how he imagined an angel would speak. Even her laugh sounded like music. *I just have to see her again.*

On Christmas Day, Tommy, his parents, and two siblings drove out to Tito and Tita's home for the big holiday gathering. As usual, it was a raucous affair with lots of laughter, a little crying, some fiery outbursts, make-up hugs, and food — tons of food. But Tommy's mind was on one thing — trying to work up the nerve to call Kristin. He had the perfect excuse. When he finally mustered the courage, he dialed her number.

"Merry Christmas, Jensen residence."

Ooh, that angelic voice. "Um, hi, Kristin? This is Tommy Segura, the guy who showed up with the baby pig. I was calling to see how he's doing."

"Hello, Tommy. The piglet is okay. My parents and I set up a pen in the barn and he slept a lot, but he's not eating anything yet. I think he's still in shock. I'd love to talk more, but we have company. You know how it is on Christmas Day."

"Oh, yeah, of course. Sorry. I, well, good-bye and merry Christmas."

He hung up the phone, shook his head, and thought, *That's the best I could say? I have to do better if I'm ever going to win her over.* The next day, he called Kristin again to check on the piglet.

"He still doesn't have an appetite, but he's improving a little bit," she reported. "I'm glad you called. You left something that my parents don't want around here — your Chicago Bears blanket. They're die-hard cheese heads."

"Would it be all right if I came over to get it?"

"I'd like that."

He punched the air with his fist in jubilation. "Great. I have to pick up some tables and chairs from my grandparents' house tomorrow afternoon, so I'll come by your place then."

They continued to talk on the phone for nearly an hour, and not once did Tommy stumble. She was sweet, charming, and witty. He hoped she thought the same of him. When he got off the phone, he couldn't stop grinning because he felt so happy. Nothing could bring him down. Absolutely nothing.

Well, almost nothing. "And the final score is Packers 16, Bears 13."

Tommy slumped on the couch in front of the TV and groaned while Manny was jumping up and down, shouting, "In your face, bro! In your face!" Manny whipped off his Green Bay jersey and handed it to Tommy. "Guess what you get to wear the first day back to school."

"The Bears should have won it," Tommy grumbled.

"Want me to go to Tito and Tita's house with you to get the table and chairs?"

"No, I can handle it alone. I couldn't stand hearing you brag the whole way about the Packers. Let me wallow in my gloom alone." *No way do I want him tagging along to Kristin's.* Looking at the Green Bay jersey, he had another thought. *Maybe this can work to my advantage.*

When Tommy showed up, Kristin greeted him with a wide-eyed smile, saying, "Well, don't you look handsome in that Packers jersey."

"I lost a bet with Manny. Besides, I was afraid your parents would shove me out the door if I showed up in Chicago blue and orange."

"Wise move."

"So how's our patient doing?"

"He still doesn't have much of an appetite, but his scrapes and cuts are healing nicely. Come see for yourself."

In the barn, the piglet was resting in a mound of hay. "My parents and I decided to keep him for good," she said. "We've named him Roadie."

Tommy got on his knees and petted the animal. From a paper bag he had brought, he pulled out two peanut butter and jelly sandwiches. "Whenever I'm feeling down, I eat a couple of these, and that always seems to perk me up." He broke off a piece and waved it in front of the piglet. "Here, Roadie, try this." The piglet got to his feet, scooted over to Tommy, and sniffed the sandwich. Then he took a bite and begged for more. In a matter of minutes, Roadie wolfed down both sandwiches and oinked in appreciation.

"You did it! You got him to eat!" Kristin shouted with glee. She threw her arms around Tommy's neck and gave him a kiss on the cheek. That did it. Tommy had fallen completely and hopelessly in love. And, as it turned out, so had Kristin.

In fact, they got married five years later, after both had graduated from the University of Illinois. Although their wedding was in June, they always made time for a private celebration on Christmas Eve — on the anniversary when Roadie the pig brought the two of them together.

The Spirit of St. Nicholas

"What a perfect day to find the perfect Christmas tree!" declared Naomi Troxler. Tilting her head skyward, she let the falling snowflakes land on her cheeks and eyelashes while her younger sister, Eva, was catching them on her tongue. The girls, ages nine and six, were standing in the middle of a sprawling Christmas tree farm in southern Michigan while their parents, Rob and Wendy, were examining a beautifully shaped white pine.

"This is pretty," said Eva. Rubbing her bare hands on the long needles, she added, "They're so soft."

"Let's not get that one," said Naomi after sniffing it. "It has no smell."

The family walked through rows of Scotch pines and Norway spruces before finding a handsome eight-foot-tall Frasier fir. "I know it's pretty," said Naomi, "but last year we got one, and the sharp needles pricked our fingers when we were decorating it. Can we please keep looking?"

Minutes later, Eva pointed to a 12-foot-tall bluish-green Canaan fir and said, "Ooh, this is a nice one."

"Oh, Eva," said Naomi, "you're always picking the tallest trees."

"A bigger tree means more room for presents," Eva countered.

"Greedy kids get coal and rocks for Christmas," said Rob with a wink. "Maybe we should get a coal bucket for you."

Eva scooped up a handful of snow, formed it into a ball, and playfully threw it at her father. Pretending to be angry, he flung a snowball in retaliation that hit her in the back. "How could you do that to such a sweet, innocent child?" Wendy said in mock outrage, firing a snowball at her husband. Suddenly, snowballs were flying through the air between the fun-loving Troxlers.

Eventually, Wendy called a truce and they resumed their search for the perfect tree. The family soon settled on an eight-foot-tall rich green balsam fir with aromatic needles that smelled like Christmas. Rob got down on his knees, began sawing, and let the girls saw, too. When the tree was finally cut down, the four of them dragged it through the snow to the edge of the field, where they were picked up by a horse-drawn wagon that was carrying two other families and their trees. On the way back to the farmhouse, everyone sang "Jingle Bells" and "The Twelve Days of Christmas."

Sure, it would have been easier to buy a precut tree at a lot in town or at a big box store. But for the Troxlers, there was something magical about weaving through rows of lush, fragrant pines, firs, and spruces in search of the right tree to cut.

At the farmhouse, the girls sipped hot chocolate while the tree was baled and put on top of their SUV. Then, with Eva tugging Naomi's hand, the sisters headed over to the farm's petting zoo, which featured a donkey, a Shetland pony, a pot-bellied pig, and several sheep, goats, and their babies. Because the girls lived on the family's small organic farm, they were comfortable around animals, especially the goats, which the Troxlers raised.

While Eva and other children were petting and feeding the animals, Naomi was drawn to a gray and black male alpine goat standing alone in the back corner of the corral behind a bale of hay. She wasn't attracted to the goat because he was cute or frisky or funny. Quite the contrary.

There's something wrong with him, she thought. He was so thin that his bones were showing, his hooves were overgrown by about four inches, and he had lost large patches of fur from mange, a skin disease. As Naomi slowly approached for a better look, the goat backed away. It was obvious he was suffering from an injury or ailment to his right front leg, because he limped badly with every step. *Oh, he's in pain. How terrible.*

"Eva! Naomi! Let's go!" shouted Rob. "The snow is really coming down now. Let's get home before the roads get too slick."

Naomi reached out and gently stroked the goat's head. Closing his big brown eyes, he moved toward her, an indication that he liked being petted.

"Naomi!"

"Coming, Daddy." Turning to the goat, she whispered, "I wish there was something I could do for you."

On the way home, Eva was chattering away about the Christmas tree and the fun she had at the farm. Naomi, though, remained quiet, her thoughts focused on the goat. *He needs medical attention and love. He needs to be rescued.*

"Naomi, is something wrong?" asked Wendy. "You've hardly said a word."

"Just thinking, Mom." *Just thinking about how to save that goat.*

When they got home, they put up the Christmas tree, which fit fine in the living room. While decorating the balsam fir with family heirloom ornaments and ones made by the girls, the Troxlers sang Christmas carols. When they were finished, Rob held Eva and climbed the stepladder. He lifted her toward the tree so she could have the honor of placing the angel on top. "There! The perfect Christmas tree!" he declared.

Yes, it is perfect, thought Naomi. But she couldn't get her mind off the goat.

The next morning, Naomi went out in the snow to tend to their family's goats and two donkeys. When she finished her chores, she returned to the house, where her mom had prepared blueberry pancakes and sausage.

Mealtime always featured interesting and lively conversation around the table in the Troxler household. Today was no different.

"Momma, Daddy," opened Naomi, "you know how you always talk about helping someone in need, especially during the holidays? Like, help thy neighbor and stuff? Well, what if that someone isn't a person?"

"What are you talking about, sweetie?" Wendy asked.

"A goat really, really needs our help."

"A goat?" asked Rob. "What goat?"

"The one at the petting zoo at the Christmas tree farm. Didn't you see him?" Her parents shook their heads. "He has mange and is super skinny and he limps. It's so sad."

"That's strange," said Rob. "I know Gus, the owner of the tree farm, and he's usually very good about the way he treats his animals. I can't imagine he would allow a goat to get in such a condition."

"The goat is going to die unless he gets rescued."

"But it's not our responsibility, sugar," Wendy said.

"Oh, really?" Naomi pulled out the Bible (the Good News Translation version) she had hidden under her chair for the specific purpose of helping her case. She flipped to a bookmarked page. "In Isaiah, Chapter 11, it says, 'Wolves and sheep will live together in peace, and leopards will lie down with young goats. Calves and lion cubs will feed together . . .'" Then, with extra emphasis on the rest of the verse, she continued, "*'and little children will take care of them.'*"

"Are you saying that you and Eva will take care of the goat?" asked Wendy.

"Yes. It's not like we don't have the room or that we don't know how to care for goats."

"She has a point, Wendy," said Rob.

"You won't have to get me anything for Christmas," said Naomi. "Just help me save the goat, please, please?"

"After church today, I have to make a delivery to the Swanburgs," said Rob. "Why don't you come with me, and we'll visit the Christmas tree farm and look into the matter."

Naomi sprang off her chair and threw her arms around her father. "Thank you, Daddy!"

When they arrived at the tree farm a few hours later, Naomi took Rob to the petting zoo and showed him the sickly, suffering goat. Rob winced at the sight and then fumed. With Naomi tailing him, he confronted the owner.

"Gus, how could you allow that goat to end up in such awful shape?"

"Rob, it's not my goat. Someone drove up Friday night while we were asleep, put it in the corral, and left. The goat is in bad condition. It's been an extremely busy weekend, so I was going to wait until tomorrow to put him down."

"No, please don't, sir!" Naomi pleaded. "Let us try to save him."

Gus smiled and nodded at her. "He's all yours, young lady, if your dad says it's okay." Looking at Rob, he added, "Your daughter must really love animals."

"Don't I know it, Gus."

On the ride home, Naomi sat in the back, petting the goat, which was lying on a blanket. "I know what we're going to call him," she told her dad. "St. Nicholas. Nick for short."

Nick was taken to the animal clinic for an examination. The vet told Naomi and her father, "The goat has several serious health issues that you could try to treat, but there's no guarantee. You might consider putting him down so he doesn't have to suffer anymore."

"But he can be treated, right?" Naomi asked.

"Possibly, with lots of care. Are you prepared to do that?"

"Yes, absolutely," Naomi replied. Turning to her father, she said, "We can't let him die, Daddy. We just can't."

He sighed. "You win, sugar, you win."

Every day for the next two months, the entire family pitched in to nurse the goat back to health. Nick, who was kept in the basement during exceptionally cold days, responded well to the medication — and to the family's love. From a sick, mangy, lame goat, he turned into a healthy, happy animal that showed undying affection toward the Troxlers, especially Naomi. He got along great with the other goats, the donkeys, and the two family dogs. However, the cat would have nothing to do with him.

Nick was a handsome *cou blanc* alpine with gray markings on his head, a white neck, white front quarters, and black hindquarters. His upright ears were dark gray, in stark contrast to his white beard.

Of all the animals on the farm — and she loved them all — Naomi had a special bond with Nick. Whenever he spotted her, he would trot over to her, nuzzle her hand, and wait to have his long, straight nose rubbed and his beard stroked. He made the weirdest bleat, a rather high-pitched *meh-meh-heh-heh* reserved only for Naomi. If any predator, like a coyote, came near the goat herd at night, Nick would let loose with a loud bleat that sounded like a boy yelling, making Nick the perfect guard goat.

As much as Nick loved to hang out with the goats and the family pets, he was attracted to birds — and they were attracted to him. His winged pals included cardinals, gold finches, cowbirds, towhees, mockingbirds, and especially mourning doves. They would circle around him and land next to him when he was resting. He'd share his feed with them and never once would he nudge them away. It wasn't uncommon to see a mourning dove perched on Nick's back.

"Other people have bird dogs," said Rob. "We have a bird goat."

Nick was an expert climber and often ended up on the roof of Rob's workshop or at the top of the highest hill on the farm. "Sometimes I see him staring at the birds," said Naomi, "and I think he wishes he could fly."

Over the years, throughout middle school and high school, Naomi remained close with Nick, who enjoyed following her around on her farm chores. She felt so comfortable with the goat that she often confided in him. If she were having some mini-crisis at school or had a crush on a boy or had a disagreement with her parents, she would talk to Nick about it. Usually, she felt better afterward — even if Nick was only a goat.

In the fall of her senior year in high school, Naomi noticed a change in Nick. He wasn't his perky self and seemed to have lost his appetite. Alarmed by his condition, she took him to the veterinarian. After a thorough examination, which included several tests, the vet gave Naomi the terrible news: Nick was dying of inoperable cancer. There was nothing that could be done.

Tears streaming down her face, Naomi asked, "How much longer does he have to live?"

"My guess is no more than a month or two. The best you could hope for is that he makes it through the holidays."

"He's been my buddy for nearly ten years. I've told him all my secrets and my dreams. He's cheered me up when I've been down. I can't imagine what it's going to be like without him in my life."

For the next six weeks, Naomi and her family did everything they could to make Nick's last days as comfortable as possible. They pampered him with special goat chow and brought him in at night when the north wind blew. Naomi's goal was to spend one more Christmas with him. But it was not to be. One evening in mid-December, she sat in the basement and cradled Nick's head in her lap as he took his final breath. The last thing he heard was her voice softly singing "Silent Night."

Nick was buried in a special plot on the Troxler property for farm animals. Naomi, Eva, Rob, and Wendy held hands and said a prayer. Overhead a flock of crows — normally loud and raucous — circled quietly as if paying somber tribute to the goat.

The next day, Naomi went into her father's workshop and made a simple wooden cross and painted Nick's name on it. She took it out to his grave, kneeled, and said, "I'm going to miss you, Nick."

While Naomi pounded the cross into the ground, a gray and brown mourning dove perched on her shoulder. Startled, she jerked to her feet. The bird took off, but it then came back and landed at Naomi's feet. It didn't look any different than the other doves. It had a long and tapered tail, a rounded head with a small dark crescent under each eye, and shiny purplish-pink patches on its neck.

Naomi bent down and stuck out her finger. The dove immediately jumped on it and stayed there as she stood up. "Well, hello there," said Naomi. "Shouldn't you be on your way to warmer weather?"

With all the bird feeders that her mother had put up on the farm, some birds chose to spend the winter here in Michigan rather than migrate south. This dove appeared to be one of them. "I have to do some chores now," Naomi said, gently flicking her finger. The dove took flight, but came right back and followed her.

When Naomi entered the barn, the dove hopped on the ground next to her. When she walked into the workshop, the bird came in through the open door. When Naomi went into the house, the bird flew to the outside sill of the kitchen window and pecked on the glass.

The next morning, Naomi fashioned a tiny wreath out of cut branches from the Christmas tree. As she walked out to Nick's grave to put the wreath on his cross, she heard the distinctive *woo-OO-oo-oo-oo* call of the mourning dove. Seconds later, the dove landed on Naomi's shoulder and stayed there while the girl hung the wreath.

Once again, the bird followed Naomi around the farm. Later, when Naomi took the car to run an errand, the dove cooed and flapped its wings as she backed out of the driveway. When Naomi returned home, the bird was waiting for her.

That evening at the dinner table, Naomi said, "The dove is attached to me and follows me everywhere. He's acting just like Nick did."

"Maybe the dove is Nick's spirit," Eva suggested.

Naomi dropped her fork as she pondered the notion. "Eva, you are *so* right!"

"Really?" said Wendy in a slightly scoffing tone. "If you think about it rationally, girls, that seems pretty far-fetched."

"You're right, Momma," Naomi conceded. "I wish it was true. It's such a wonderful thought: that Nick's spirit is still with us in the form of a dove."

The temperature had plunged into the teens, causing Naomi to worry about the bird. Before going to bed, she got a blanket, fluffed it up, and put it on the chair swing that hung in the back porch near the kitchen window. The next morning, she found the dove sleeping on the blanket, its head resting between its shoulders.

Every day for the next week, the bird patiently waited for Naomi to step outside and then followed her around. At night, it slept on the blanket.

On Christmas morning, Eva opened the door to let the dogs out. She shrieked when the mourning dove swooped inside, took one spin around the living room, and landed on a branch near the top of the tree.

"I guess the dove wants to say merry Christmas," said Eva. "Can he stay for a while, Mommy?"

"Sure, sure he can."

So the Troxlers opened their presents while the dove cooed and watched from above. The last gift under the tree was for Nick. Naomi had bought it and wrapped it just days before she had learned her beloved goat was dying. Unwrapping the box, she took out a handcrafted leather collar. "I might as well give it to one of the other goats," she said.

Suddenly, the dove fluttered down from the tree and perched right on Naomi's head, causing everyone to laugh. Naomi held out her index finger, and the dove hopped on it. "You really *are* Nick's spirit," she beamed.

Just then, the dogs began barking to be let in. When Naomi opened the door, the dove took off. This time it didn't roost in the tree or on the roof or windowsill. No, it kept circling higher and higher until it was a speck against the Columbia blue sky. Then it banked to the south and flew away.

Naomi had a feeling the dove was never coming back, and she was okay with that. She believed Nick's spirit had shared one more Christmas with her, and no one was going to convince her otherwise.

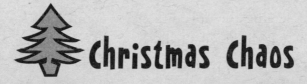

Christmas Chaos

Submerged from their necks down in their hot tub, Paige Zeller and her husband, Drew, leaned against each other. Both were mentally and physically exhausted. Neither spoke for several minutes while reliving in their minds the stressful but wacky events earlier in the day.

As the steam swirled around them in the chilly night air, Drew broke the silence. "There has never been a Christmas quite like this one."

"Not even close," Paige agreed. "I should have known this wouldn't be an ordinary holiday the moment Charlie nearly drowned."

"I figured it couldn't get any crazier after Max toppled the Christmas tree."

"But we hadn't counted on Charlie's and Max's other shenanigans."

"The topper, though, was the way Chloe embarrassed Poppy."

"That, Drew, was priceless."

"Mark it in your diary: 'Christmas 1993 — the day the pets sabotaged our family gathering.'"

＊ ＊ ＊

Even though the Zellers lived in balmy south Florida, Paige did her best to bring the festive Christmas spirit into their spacious upscale home for Drew and their sons, Aiden, 15; Noah, 13; and Carter, 5. Everyone had a role in the decorating, which took place the week after Thanksgiving. The first task for Drew and the boys was to bring down the boxes — there were more than two dozen — of decorations from the attic.

Then Paige took over. She replaced her collection of dainty seashells, large conch shells, and framed sand dollars with her collection of expensive Santa figures. Some Santas were carved out of wood or made out of clay. But the ones she prized the most were the Santas with hand-painted resin faces, inset glass eyes, real mohair beards, and clothing made from imported tapestry, velvet, satin, suede, and leather.

During Christmas decorating time, Charlie — the family's African gray parrot — joined in the holiday spirit with his own comments. His two favorites: "Deck the halls, deck the halls, squawk!" and "Santa Claus is coming, watch out!" The ten-year-old bird had an excellent vocabulary and could mimic such electronic sounds as the microwave, telephone, alarm clock, and even the kids' video games.

From his cage in the family room, which flowed into the open kitchen and out to the screened-in pool area, he watched Paige set down various figurines of Frosty the Snowman, the Grinch, and Santa's elves. He sat on her shoulder when she dressed up the rooms in greenery, with fake but realistic-looking holly, garland, and mistletoe. She hung six large handmade stockings on the marble fireplace mantle for the family, including Charlie.

Drew and the boys were responsible for putting up the outdoor lights along the rooflines, around the front windows, and along the gardenia shrubs. Being especially ambitious this year, they strung hundreds of lights on the two big palm trees in the front yard. Of course, they didn't dare forget to put out the four-foot-tall outdoor-lighted plastic Santa and snowman at each end of the pool deck. To finish off the outdoor decorations, they tossed an inflatable three-foot-tall elf into the pool.

Getting the Christmas tree and decorating it was always a big production for the Zellers. This year, the family went to the bustling souvenir store/soda shop, where everyone had to pick out a holiday T-shirt to wear to the Christmas tree lot. The store was owned by Drew's father, Tony, whom the kids called Poppy. Carter chose a T-shirt that boasted SANTA LOVES ME BEST. Noah selected one that read DEAR SANTA . . . LET ME EXPLAIN. Aiden donned a T-shirt that pictured two peapods standing on top of a globe with the words PEAS ON EARTH. Drew decided on one showing a snowman in sunglasses, beach hat, and swimming trunks that read JUST CHILLIN', while Paige — the most sentimental one in the family — chose a shirt that said DON'T STOP BELIEVING.

At their favorite Christmas tree lot, they debated for nearly 30 minutes before agreeing on a magnificent ten-foot-tall Frasier fir. Back home, they secured it in the tree stand in their living room. Then Paige played holiday music and, like a battlefield commander, directed Drew and the boys on where to place the lights and ornaments. Charlie, who was perched on Aiden's shoulder during the tree trimming, occasionally shouted, "Ho! Ho! Ho! Merry, merry!"

When it was all done, the Zellers stepped back and admired the tree. "It's so beautiful, so Christmassy." Paige beamed.

"Now, if we only had snow outside, it'd be outstanding," said Noah.

Drew turned to Paige and said, "Everything looks super. So, how many are we having for Christmas dinner?"

"At last count it's seventeen," she replied. Accepting invitations were her brother, Nat, and his wife, Barb, who were driving from their home in Virginia; her sister, Kay, and Kay's 12-year-old twins, Rachel and Robyn; Drew's father, Tony, and Tony's girlfriend, Brooke; and Drew's brother, Mike, his wife, Cindy, and their kids, Mike Jr., 14; Andi, 13; and Anthony, 8. "The main table can hold twelve, and we'll put the five youngest around the kitchen table," Paige said.

"Here's wishing everyone is on their best behavior," said Drew. "I don't want a repeat of last year, when Kay and Cindy got snippy with each other. . . ."

"And you had some icy words with Brooke."

Charlie interrupted, "Watch out! Santa Claus is coming! Squawk! Watch out!"

From the kitchen, Noah blurted an angry yell and began chasing Aiden into the family room and out the open sliding-glass door to the pool.

"What's going on?" Drew demanded.

"Aiden put ice down my back!" Noah shouted back.

"I was just trying to give him a feel for the snow he wanted," Aiden explained a split second before Noah shoved him in the pool.

"Fight! Fight!" squawked Charlie, his favorite words whenever the boys were squabbling.

❄ ❄ ❄

A few days before Christmas, Paige and Carter decided to add color to the tree by making strings of cranberries and mini marshmallows and strings of cranberries and popcorn. While they were crafting the edible decorations to drape around the tree, Charlie stood on the kitchen counter and ate all the loose cranberries.

Later that day, Nat and Barb arrived for a week's stay with the Zellers. The boys fondly called Nat "Uncle Nut" after Noah kept mispronouncing his name when the boy was a toddler. The name stuck because nutty things seemed to happen to Nat — mostly by his own doing. Although the kids found him funny, Charlie didn't like him and never did, for no apparent reason.

"African grays are among the smartest birds in the world, so maybe there's a good reason why Charlie doesn't like Uncle Nut," cracked Aiden.

On Christmas morning, after presents were opened and breakfast was finished, Barb and Drew helped Paige with the early preparations for the big dinner later in the day. The older boys played video games while Nat showed Carter some card tricks out by the pool. Charlie watched from his cage nearby.

When Carter got bored with the cards, Nat told him, "I'm going to make friends with Charlie."

As Nat started to open the cage, Charlie squawked, "Nutso! Nutso!"

"Um, Uncle Nut," said Carter, "Momma told you not to let him out."

"Nonsense. Watch this." Nat opened the cage and, with

a piece of cantaloupe, coaxed Charlie to climb on his finger. "See? I'm not so bad after all," Nat said to the parrot as the bird nibbled on the cantaloupe. "We're pals now, right?"

Charlie responded by digging his sharp talons around Nat's finger.

"Yeow!" Nat shouted in pain. "Let go, you idiot bird!"

When the parrot continued to hang on, Nat tried to shake him off. But the more Nat waved his hand, the more Charlie dug in. Uttering a few choice, angry words, Nat violently jerked his hand until he flung the bird off. Unfortunately for Charlie — who couldn't fly because his wings had been clipped — he landed smack in the middle of the pool.

Squawking in panic, Charlie flapped his wings, but all he could do was turn in circles. Seeing the parrot in distress, Nat stripped down to his underwear and jumped into the pool. When he reached Charlie, the crazed bird tried to bite him. "For crying out loud, you stupid parrot, I'm trying to save your life!" snarled Nat.

Finally, Nat grabbed the bird and treaded toward the shallow end. Having heard the commotion, Paige, Drew, Barb, and the older boys had rushed to the pool steps. When Nat handed Charlie to Paige, she was swinging between two emotions — concern and fury. "Oh, Charlie, my little baby!" she cooed before launching into a tirade at her brother. "How could you, Nat? I told you not to let him out. But noooo, you had to ignore me. Now see what you've caused?" She grabbed a towel and wrapped it around the shivering parrot. Then she stomped off.

"Uh, could someone get me a towel, please?" asked Nat as he stepped out of the pool. Seeing their dripping wet, overweight uncle in white briefs made the boys wince. Aiden quickly tossed him a towel.

By the time Charlie — and Paige, for that matter — had calmed down, the doorbell rang. In walked Poppy and his much younger companion, Brooke. After trading kisses and hugs with the others, Poppy said, "Paige, I hope you don't mind, but I've brought a guest."

"Oh, who?" she asked.

"He's in the car. I'll get him." Moments later, he returned with a young brown and black German shepherd. "His name is Max. He's eight months old, housebroken, and very obedient."

"You could have told us you were bringing a dog," said Paige.

"Sorry. It slipped my mind."

"Isn't he just divine?" gushed Brooke. "Tony got him a couple of weeks ago from a friend who was recovering from a heart attack and couldn't care for Max anymore. Max is an early Christmas present for me. He's a sweetie pie — Max, that is . . . and Tony, too."

Paige rolled her eyes and went back to work in the kitchen. "Nutso!" Charlie chirped. "Nutso!"

After Mike and his family arrived, everyone gathered around the pool area where they munched on raw veggies and dip, a cheese ball and crackers, sliced sausage, deviled eggs, and chilled shrimp.

While Nat was telling the guests about his heroic rescue of Charlie, they heard a crash — a loud thud followed by popping and breaking glass — in the living room. "That didn't sound good," said Nat in an understatement.

They hurried into the living room, where some gasped in surprise, others giggled, and the rest were left speechless. The tree had fallen over onto the ceramic tile floor, shattering several ornaments and decorations, and crushing many lightbulbs.

"Oh . . . my . . . God!" moaned Paige, pressing her hands against her cheeks in dismay. "Tell me I'm having a bad dream."

"I could tell you that, but it wouldn't be the truth," Drew said. "It's more like a real-life nightmare."

The tree hadn't fallen on its own. It had been pulled down. And no one had to guess who did it; they all knew. Max was scrunched in the opposite corner of the room, where a long string of marshmallows and cranberries dangled from his mouth.

Brooke hurried over to the dog and hugged him. "Oh, Max, are you all right? Did that big bad tree fall on you?"

Getting steamed because Brooke cared more about the dog than the mess he had created, Paige growled, "Your dog is fine. The tree is not fine. And I am not fine." Turning to her father-in-law, she said, "Poppy, you're in charge of getting this all cleaned up."

Kay and the twins couldn't have picked a worse time to arrive. "Hey, everybody," Kay bellowed, "merry Chris —" She stopped when she saw broken ornaments and the fallen tree on the floor. Surveying the scene, she joked, "Did somebody get a chainsaw for Christmas?"

"Somebody — I won't mention any names — brought over an uninvited dog, who took such a liking to our cranberry and marshmallow decorations that he decided to taste the fruits of our labor," said Paige sarcastically. "He yanked so hard, he pulled down the tree."

Trying to minimize the situation, Kay said, "Everything will be fine, sis. What's a Christmas without a few broken ornaments, anyway?" She went over to Paige and gave her a kiss. "I know you're frazzled, so maybe it'll be best to keep Chloe in the bathroom."

"Chloe? Who's Chloe?"

"Our new cat, Aunt Paige," said Rachel, opening the bright yellow beach bag she was carrying to reveal a tan and brown two-year-old American shorthair. "We got her from the shelter last week."

"Please don't lock her in the bathroom," pleaded Robyn. "She'll be good. We'll hold her. Please?"

Paige threw her hands in the air and sighed. "Why not? What more could happen?"

The tree was put back in its stand, the unbroken ornaments were re-hung on the branches, and the mess was swept up. Then everyone returned to the pool patio and resumed eating the appetizers. A few minutes later, Paige and Kay went into the master bedroom to take a call from their brother, who was in the Air Force on the other side of the world.

Drew had just stepped into the kitchen for more ice when he heard the timer on the oven beeping rather loudly. Rather than disturb Paige, he pulled out the 20-pound turkey, set it on the counter to cool, and turned off the timer and the stove. Because of the way the day was going, he didn't want any further mishaps, such as having the dog or cat take a bite out of the turkey. So he set it out of reach on top of the refrigerator.

"Ho! Ho! Ho! Merry, merry!" cackled Charlie, who was enjoying some peace and quiet in his cage in the family room while recovering from his near-death experience.

About a half hour before the planned 5:30 dinner, Paige and Drew came into the kitchen to complete the final preparations. She opened the oven and gasped, "What in the world?"

"Oh, I took the turkey out at about four when the timer went off," Drew replied, carefully returning the turkey to the counter.

"But I set the timer to go off at five," said Paige. She cut into the turkey and groaned. "It's not done yet. It needs another hour to cook. Drew, you took it out way too soon."

"I swear the timer went off at four." Seconds later, they heard beeping. "That's the sound of the timer. Hey, that's strange, because the timer isn't on. So what are we hearing?"

"Oh, no! It's Charlie!" Paige exclaimed. "He's mimicking the sound of the kitchen timer. That's what you heard earlier. He unwittingly tricked you into taking out the turkey before it was done." Turning to the parrot, she said, "Charlie, of all the sounds you imitate, why did you choose today to mimic the kitchen timer? Argh!"

As she put the turkey back in the oven and set the timer, Paige was on the verge of tears. "Between the bird and the dog, this day is turning into a disaster," she complained to Drew.

"I wonder what surprise the *cat* has for us," Drew joked. Seeing that Paige wasn't amused, he put his arm around her and reassured her, "Everything is going to be all right. This family is used to having crazy things happen."

Calming down, Paige returned to the pool area. "Folks," she told her guests, "dinner is going to be delayed about an hour, because Charlie tried to sabotage our holiday feast. I guess he doesn't want us eating a fellow bird."

The guests all took the news with good humor. It was worth the wait. When dinner was served, they dug into the whipped mashed potatoes and gravy, green bean casserole, sausage stuffing, cranberry sauce, tossed salad, rolls, and of course, turkey. The conversation was lively and punctuated often by laughter.

As for the pets, Charlie was quiet; Max was under the kids' table, catching everything that fell and begging for more; and Chloe was curled up on the couch in the family room.

After everyone ate more than they should have, they decided to hold off on the pumpkin pie. While several guests helped Paige clean up, the rest went into the family room to watch football. Poppy sat down on the couch near the sleeping cat and within ten minutes was dozing.

Relieved there had been no crises during dinner, Paige began to relax. The guests in the kitchen were having a good laugh over the mishaps from earlier in the day. "Well, at least my cat didn't cause any problems," crowed Kay.

During the cleanup, Max trotted into the kitchen. Seeing an open garbage bag on the floor, the dog stuck his nose in and pulled out a turkey leg. "Max, no!" shouted Paige. "You'll choke on that bone! Drop it!"

Rather than release the bone, Max tried to flee, but his paws kept slipping on the slick ceramic tile floor before they got traction. With the bone still in his mouth, he dashed for the family room, which was also tiled. Seeing Paige and Aiden chase after him, Max tried to turn so he could run out through the open sliding-glass door to the pool deck. But he slid out of control, slamming into the couch. That freaked out Chloe. In a panic, the cat leaped on Poppy's head and bounded off onto a high bookcase shelf behind him. She arched her back, hissed, and accidentally knocked off a ceramic Santa that crashed to the floor in pieces. Meanwhile, Aiden tackled Max and wrested the turkey leg out of the dog's mouth.

But that's not what caused the biggest shock. When Chloe sprang from Poppy's noggin, she dislodged his hairpiece — one that no one knew he wore — and caused it to slide down over his left ear, exposing his bald spot. Blushing redder than a papaya, Poppy hurriedly tried to adjust the hairpiece.

At first, no one knew how to react. They all stared at Paige for a cue. It was one of those special moments in life when Paige had to make a split-second choice between laughing or crying. She chose laughing, and burst into

guffaws, triggering a round of hysterics that left everyone —
including Poppy — gasping for breath and holding their
sides. Those who were standing had slumped to the floor,
and those who were sitting had doubled over. Every time
the laughter started to die down, someone would giggle,
reigniting a new series of laughs.

"Congratulations, Paige," said Kay. "No one will ever
top this Christmas!"

"No offense, Mom," said Aiden, "but the credit shouldn't
go to you. It should go to the ones who caused all the
mayhem — Charlie, Max, and Chloe."

 # Coonhound Surprise

Dear Santa Claus,
I have been a good girl. My brother isn't very nice and pulls my hair. Can you give me a princess dress? You can bring a pail of stones for my brother.
Love,
Etta

Sofia Westlake giggled and then read the note out loud to her mother, Tilly. The two of them were trading laughs while sifting through letters to Santa collected at the local post office where Tilly worked. Every year for the past three years, the Westlakes would select two letters from the neediest kids and fulfill their wishes.

Some of the requests were heartbreaking and beyond their reach, such as, "Can you make Dad be nice to Mom?" or "Please bring my sister home from the hospital. I miss her very much."

Sofia, 14, reached into the small pile on the dining room table and pulled out another letter.

Dear Santa,

I am nine years old. My mom and dad are great people and work hard and buy nice things for me and my brothers and grandma. They never buy anything for themselves. My wish for Christmas is that you bring my mom a warm sweater and bring my dad new work boots.

Thank you,

Cody

"We can help this kid," declared Sofia.

Tilly replied, "Put it in the 'yes, we will' folder." The letter joined another one from a disabled girl whose only request was toys for her siblings. With five days to go before Christmas, the Westlakes were gearing up to bring joy to two deserving families.

Sofia beamed and said, "Mom, have I told you how much I love this time of year?"

❄ ❄ ❄

A week earlier, eight-year-old Kyle Gabbert hopped out of the car and did a little two-step in the Texas dirt. "I can't believe we're getting a puppy for Christmas!" he shouted gleefully, bounding up to the front door of the Fairfield Animal Shelter. He was followed by his two younger sisters, Jolene and Luella, and his mother, Hanna.

Once inside, the girls were angling to get one of the smaller breeds, such as the Chihuahua or Pomeranian mix. But Kyle nixed those suggestions. "They yip and yap. I want a *real* dog."

There were several mongrels that seemed friendly. The kids picked out a female beagle mix and took her into a room to see how she interacted with them. Possibly intimidated by three kids trying to hug her all at once, the dog backed up and growled. "She's scared," said Hanna. "Kyle, put her on a leash and walk with her and see how she does." He did, but it didn't go well, either.

The kids tried to bond with a terrier, but he was way too hyper, knocking over Jolene and sticking his tongue in Luella's face, causing her to cry.

"Well, that didn't work out," said Hanna. "Let's go back and look at some other dogs."

Kyle walked over to the cage of a sleeping white hound that he had ignored during the previous pass-throughs. The dog was lying on his side with his back to the cage. Kyle reached through the bars and petted him. The hound rolled on his back and gave a contented sigh and opened his eyes. Then he sat up and licked Kyle's hand.

"Could I play with this one?" he asked his mother.

"Are you sure you want to? He looks kind of old and not very cute."

Marnie, the shelter volunteer said, "He was brought in

a couple of weeks ago. Animal control found him hanging around the grocery store on Noble Avenue. We think he's abandoned. Not sure how old he is, but I guess he's two or three."

"Please, can I play with him?" Kyle asked.

The white dog gave a little wag with his tail. Once in the room, he let the girls pet him and didn't shy away. When he licked them, he did it slowly as if offering them the opportunity to move out of range, which they didn't. All the while, though, he kept his eyes on Kyle. When the boy jogged around the room, the dog followed him. When Kyle sat on the floor, the dog plopped down next to him. When Kyle petted him, the dog rubbed his head under the boy's chin.

"Mom, he's the one I want for Christmas. Can we get him, please?"

Even the girls were in agreement. "Yes, can we, Mommy?"

"Well, okay."

"Yippee!" shouted the girls.

Kyle gave his mother a big hug. "Thanks, Mom. I've already got a name picked out — Boomer."

With the kids by her side, Hanna filled out a form and answered several questions from the shelter director, Mrs. Davis: Will you provide your pet the necessary medical attention, including yearly checkups? Will you commit to caring for your pet for 10 to 15 years? Will you consent to a visit by a member of our staff? Hanna answered "yes" to all the questions.

Kyle was getting more excited by the minute, telling his sisters, "Boomer will soon be ours!"

Hanna reached into her purse and pulled out her wallet. "How much is it going to cost?"

"Two hundred dollars," said Mrs. Davis.

"What? For a dog nobody else wants?" Hanna challenged. "That's mighty expensive."

"Actually, it's a bargain," Mrs. Davis explained. "The money goes for neutering, grooming, putting in a microchip in case he's lost, vaccinations, deworming, anti-flea-and-tick application, and a thorough medical examination by a vet. Not a single penny of the adoption fee is used for the shelter's overhead or administrative costs."

Hanna counted the money in her wallet and then put it back in her purse. "I simply can't afford it right now," she admitted. "I'm a single parent with a decent job as a secretary, but it's still hard to make ends meet, especially at this time of year."

"I understand," Mrs. Davis replied. "I'm sorry. I wish there was something I could do."

Kyle felt his stomach twist into a knot. The happy

anticipation of getting Boomer had swiftly turned into crushing disappointment.

"I've got about ten dollars in my piggy bank," he offered, knowing full well it wasn't close to enough. His shoulders slumped when his mother shook her head.

"I feel terrible because there's nothing more I can do," she said. "We're one hundred dollars short. Maybe after all the Christmas bills are paid . . ."

Kyle turned to Mrs. Davis and asked, "What about Boomer? What's going to happen to him?"

The director hesitated. "We keep the animals as long as we can, and then when new animals arrive, we have to make room for them, so . . ."

Kyle then said what she didn't want to say in front of the children. "You put the older ones to sleep," he snapped. Softening his tone, he begged, "Please, ma'am, not Boomer. Wait till we can get the money."

"I'll keep him as long as we can, maybe up to Christmas," replied Mrs. Davis. "But I can't promise anything."

On the ride home, Kyle wiped away the tears and repeatedly muttered, "There's got to be a way." As they passed the mall, he noticed the electronic marquee was flashing Santa's visiting hours. Suddenly, Kyle perked up. "Mom, I know how we can get the money."

❄ ❄ ❄

Sofia and her mother took a look at the remaining two letters on the dining room table to see if either request was more worthy than the two they had already selected.

Sofia picked up one that was colorfully addressed in red and green crayon to "Santa Claus, North Pole."

Dear Santa,
Can I have hamburgers and French fries every day?
Your good friend,
Jason

"Nope," said Sofia. "But I am getting hungry."
Tilly opened the last envelope:

Dear Santa Claus,
Thank you very much for the presents last year. This year I would like to have twice as many. You know what I like.
Love,
Theresa

"Well, she's out," said Tilly. "It's decided, then. We have our two families."

This year, the Westlakes set their budget at $200, and it looked like it would take all of it — and then some — to buy all the toys and clothes requested in the two letters.

As they cleared the table, Sofia spotted an unopened envelope that had fallen unnoticed under her chair. She read it:

Dear Santa:
Me and my mom were looking for a puppy for Christmas. We wanted to get a shelter dog. There was a white dog in a cage, and he was sleeping. When I petted him, he woke up and rolled over and licked my hand. Mom said we could take him home. But the shelter says we need two hundred dollars to take him to the dog hospital to get fixed. Mom has only one hundred dollars. Can you bring me one hundred dollars for Christmas, so Boomer could be my dog?
Thank you,
Kyle

"Mom, we're going to help *three* families this year," Sofia announced.

After reading the letter, Tilly wasn't sure, saying, "But we'll go way over our budget."

"Don't worry. I have it all figured out . . . and it won't cost us a dime."

❄ ❄ ❄

Every day for a week, Kyle called Mrs. Davis at the shelter to make sure that Boomer was still there. And every day he was reassured that, yes, Boomer hadn't been adopted or put to sleep. With Christmas less than a week away, Mrs. Davis was getting annoyed with Kyle and asked to speak to his mother.

She told Hanna, "I wish your son wouldn't call anymore. I don't want to be the one who has to tell him later this week, 'Sorry, the dog was just put down.'"

"Please delay it as long as you can," Hanna pleaded. "I'll get the money."

Hearing his mother's end of the conversation, Kyle knew time was running out. "If they can just keep Boomer alive until Christmas, I know Santa will bring us the money," he said. "Last year I asked for a bike, and Santa got me one."

Hanna had bought him a used bike and cleaned it and touched it up with paint so it looked new. She wanted to do something special for him again this year. *Kyle is such a good boy*, she thought. *He helps around the house and never complains and is so good with the girls. He deserves this one present. But where am I going to get an extra hundred dollars?*

Her answer came at the office Christmas party. Her boss, Mr. Kurtz, took her aside and said, "Hanna, I want you to know how much I appreciate your hard work. Business has been slow, so I can't give bonuses to all my employees. But you are the exception. I'm giving you a twenty-five-dollar-a-week raise . . . and this." He handed her an envelope. She opened it to find a holiday greeting card with a crisp new one-hundred-dollar bill.

"Oh, Mr. Kurtz, thank you, thank you! This couldn't have come at a better time. With this bonus, you'll be making one boy and one hound dog very happy."

Hanna rushed home and told Kyle and the girls, "Guess what? One of Santa's elves dropped off a special gift to us!"

"What is it? What is it?" the girls asked.

"Money to bring Boomer home with us!" she announced, waving the hundred-dollar bill.

Kyle jumped for joy. "I knew Santa would answer my letter! I just knew it!"

The family arrived at the shelter ten minutes before closing. "I have the money for the adoption of Boomer," Hanna told Mrs. Davis.

Kyle didn't wait for all the details to be worked out. He was so excited that he dashed to the back where the dogs were caged and shouted, "Boomer! Boomer! I'm here!" He ran over to the cage where the dog was kept and skidded to a stop. His heart sank. The cage was empty.

Thinking they had moved the dog, he started calling Boomer's name, checking every cage, many of them occupied by new strays. Now fearing the worst, he slumped to the floor and thought, *Is he in doggy heaven?*

Bursting into tears, he got up and barged into Mrs. Davis's office. "Where's Boomer?" he demanded.

"Well, as I was explaining to your mother, he's not here. He's . . ."

Kyle didn't need to hear any more. *I know what happened.* Bawling, Kyle flew out the door, ran over to a bench, and buried his head in his hands. "How could they kill Boomer?"

In his grief, he failed to see a car pull up and a teenage girl and her mother get out. He also failed to see who else got out.

A few minutes later, the girl came over and said, "Hi, I'm Sofia. Mind if I sit down?"

Kyle rubbed his runny nose with the back of his hand and shrugged.

"You look sad," she said. "What's wrong?"

"There was this hound dog, and I wanted to adopt him, only we didn't have enough money. I asked Santa for a hundred dollars and — this is true — an elf gave my mom a hundred dollars, and I was sure I'd get the dog. But" — his voice choked as he pointed to the animal shelter — "they killed him."

"That's not true," Sofia said.

"Uh-huh. Everything I said is true."

"Not exactly everything. Turn around."

He wiped the tears from his eyes and looked back toward the shelter. Once again, he began crying, only this time out of sheer happiness. Standing outside the door were his mother, sisters, Mrs. Davis, Hanna, and . . . "Oh wow, oh wow, oh wow! Boomer! You're alive!"

Hanna let go of the dog's leash. Boomer sprinted over to Kyle, who had dropped to his knees, and covered the boy's face with slobbery kisses.

"Merry Christmas, Kyle," said Sofia.

❄ ❄ ❄

Sofia felt proud, darned proud, for pulling off this surprise. Here's how she did it:

The day after she had read Kyle's letter to Santa, she walked into the Spring Hill Animal Clinic, which was run by Dr. Miguel Guerrero, the father of her best friend, Maria. Handing him the letter, Sofia asked, "Can you help, Dr. Guerrero? It would mean so much to the boy and the dog . . . and it is Christmas."

"How can I say no?" replied the vet. "We need to get that boy's dog ready for adoption. Christmas is only three days away."

After confirming the hound was still at the shelter, Tilly and Sofia picked up Boomer and brought him to Dr. Guerrero's clinic. The vet gave Boomer his health exam — he was in good health — vaccinated him, and checked him for worms and heartworms. Then the dog was neutered.

Late in the afternoon on the following day, Sofia and her mother arrived at the clinic to pick up the dog and take him back to the shelter. As the vet handed Boomer over to them, he said, "One Christmas wish is about to come true. If it hadn't been for Kyle's letter and for you two, this three-year-old hound mix had about a zero chance of being adopted. He would have been put down. He literally got the break of his life."

Sofia and her mother returned the dog to the shelter shortly after Kyle and his family arrived. While Kyle was crying on the bench, the Westlakes went into the office with Boomer, bringing an unexpected thrill to Hanna and the girls.

"I can't thank you enough for preparing the dog for adoption," Hanna told the Westlakes. "Do I pay you or the shelter for the vet bill?"

"You don't owe anyone anything," Sofia replied. "It's all taken care of, courtesy of Dr. Guerrero and the Spring Hill Animal Clinic. So, merry Christmas! Now, let's go surprise Kyle."

Moments later, as they watched Kyle embrace Boomer, Sofia said, "Mom, have I told you how much I love this time of year?"

Smokey's Holiday Adventure

"Meghan, did you take my charm bracelet?" Erin asked her sister.

"No. Why would I want to?"

"Because you're always 'borrowing' my things without asking," replied Erin, forming quote marks with her fingers.

"Maybe if you gave back the beaded necklace that I lent you, I'd help you find your precious charm bracelet."

"I *did* give your necklace back," Erin insisted. "I put it right on the table next to your bed."

"No, you didn't."

"Yes, I did."

The McCleary sisters — 12-year-old Meghan was a year older than Erin — were bickering more than usual, testing the patience of their divorced mother, Valerie. The breakup of her marriage was combative, causing an emotional toll on her and the girls. Now, facing the first Christmas without a husband, Valerie was trying to reduce the stress that had plagued everyone, including the girls' grandfather, in whose house they lived.

"How about as a Christmas present, you girls get me something that won't cost you anything?" Valerie suggested.

"What's that, Mom?" Meghan asked.

"For you two not to argue with each other from now until the end of the year."

"But, that's like for three whole weeks," Erin complained. "Really, Mom? Really? Three weeks without Meghan starting a fight? Impossible."

"Me starting a fight?" Meghan protested. "You're the one who —"

"Enough! Erin, help set the dinner table. Meghan, go turn on the Christmas lights and check the water level for the Christmas tree."

After plugging in the outdoor lights and Christmas tree lights, Meghan poured water into the tree holder. Noticing a couple of bulbs were flickering, she leaned into the tree to tighten them in their sockets. Suddenly, her gaze focused on two golden eyes staring at her from inside the tree. "Aaaah!" Meghan yelped, backing away.

Then she began giggling. "Smokey, is that you in there?" Hearing a *meow*, Meghan reached in and pulled out the family's coal-black Bombay cat. Holding him up under his front legs, she said, "Smokey, this is a Christmas tree, not a climbing tree." She put him down, gave him a shove, and said, "Scoot, scoot."

Returning to the tree, Meghan finished fixing the bulbs when her eye caught something sparkle where Smokey had been. She reached in and pulled out Erin's missing charm bracelet, which had been resting on a junction of two inner branches. "I don't believe it!" she murmured.

Just then Erin walked into the room. "Ah-ha! See? I knew you took the bracelet! I caught you red-handed."

"I found it in the tree."

"Yeah, right," Erin scoffed.

"Smokey was in there, too. He must have taken it."

"Now you're blaming the cat? You can make up a better story than that, Meghan."

"It's the truth."

"I see," Erin said sarcastically. She stuck her hand in the tree and said, "You just happened to reach into the tree like this, and you just happened —"

Erin stopped talking when her fingers felt something dangling from a nub jutting out of the tree trunk. When she withdrew the object, she was surprised to see it was Meghan's necklace.

"Now do you believe me?" snapped Meghan, snatching the necklace out of her sister's hand. "I told you it was Smokey."

That night at the dinner table, the family had a good laugh over Smokey's thefts. They needed some levity because, in addition to the divorce, they were still getting over their grief from the loss of their other family cat. A week earlier, Smokey's pal Cumquat, a tan and black Persian, had to be put down.

"Smokey has been getting into more mischief lately," said Valerie. "I found him batting around one of my earrings on the bathroom floor."

"Remember the other night, he knocked over my glass of water on the nightstand?" said the girls' grandfather, whom they called Peepaw. "Yesterday he got into the kitchen garbage can, and I had to yank him out by the scruff of the neck."

"I wonder if he's acting up because he misses Cumquat," said Valerie.

"Well," said Meghan, "if anything is missing, we'll know who to blame."

Smokey and Cumquat were best pals who had been together since before the girls were born. They slept together, usually with a family member. One night it would be with Erin; another at the foot of Valerie's bed; one night under the covers with Meghan; another under Peepaw's bed. Sometimes they'd spend three straight nights with one of the McClearys and then not sleep with them again for a week or two. You just never knew with those two.

But ever since Cumquat's death, Smokey had been roaming the house at night, choosing new places to sleep. "I wonder if he's searching for Cumquat," said Meghan.

About two weeks before Christmas, the family was having dinner when Erin asked, "Has anyone seen Smokey today? I put food in his bowl this morning, and I just noticed it hasn't been touched."

Peepaw last spotted him trying to swipe a piece of bacon off the breakfast table. Meghan had shooed the cat out of her closet while getting ready for school. Valerie remembered seeing Smokey bat at her mop while she was cleaning the kitchen floor that morning.

"You don't think he's dead from a broken heart, do you?" asked Erin. "Cats are known to find a hiding place to die."

"Oh, Erin, quit being so dramatic," Meghan muttered.

After dinner, the McClearys scoured the house looking for Smokey, checking the Christmas tree; under the couch, easy chairs, and beds; in the closets; behind the pillows; and even in the lower kitchen cabinets. There was no sign of the cat.

"Did anyone leave the door open?" Meghan asked.

"Yes, I did," said Valerie. "I had propped it open when Peepaw and I were bringing in the groceries from the car at lunchtime. Smokey could have sneaked outside then. He's done it before."

"But he never strays far from the house," said Meghan. "He hates the outdoors."

"And he always meows to be let in."

Armed with flashlights, the four of them went outside to look for Smokey. Meghan said out loud what everyone else was thinking: "How do you find a black cat in the dark?"

They searched in the bushes around the house, checked the garage, and looked in the family cars. Splitting into two-person teams, the McClearys walked up and down the neighborhood streets, calling Smokey's name. After three futile hours, the family called it quits for the night.

"At least he's wearing his collar and tags, so if someone finds him, they'll call us," Peepaw said.

The next day, Valerie phoned the neighbors, asking if they had seen the cat. She checked with the emergency animal hospital and the local animal shelter. No Smokey. After school, Meghan and Erin made up "lost cat" flyers. Then they hopped on their bikes and plastered the notices on light posts, telephone poles, walls, and the post office's community bulletin board.

Every day, the girls roamed the neighborhood, asking everyone they saw if they had spotted Smokey. After yet another unsuccessful search, Erin told her sister, "I think he's dead."

"No," Meghan said. "He's alive. I'm sure of it."

The flyers drew a few calls that proved to be false alarms. Valerie was the first to give up. She told the girls, "It's been two weeks, and no one has seen Smokey. We'll wait until Christmas and then take down the flyers. We'll assume he has joined Cumquat."

On Christmas Eve, the McClearys gathered by the tree. They sipped eggnog and, following a family tradition, each opened a single present. Before Erin opened her gift, she said, "If I had one wish, it would be that Smokey was here with us."

"Remember the time Mrs. Kranepool stopped by with her German shepherd and Smokey hissed at him and he cowered and peed all over the front step?" Megan recalled.

"Or when he leaped onto the fireplace mantle and knocked off that ugly vase that Aunt Jenny had given Mom?" added Erin.

Valerie giggled. "We all cheered."

"Yeah, and you cheered the loudest," Meghan said.

Peepaw piped in, "Let's not forget when Smokey and Cumquat —"

He was interrupted by the telephone ringing. Meghan went into the kitchen and answered it. "Hello," said a young male voice in a thick country drawl. "Uh, are you missin' a black cat?"

Meghan held her breath in anticipation. "Yes, yes we are. Have you found him?"

"I think so. My buddy an' I saw a black cat wanderin' 'round in a Burger King parkin' lot. He was meowin' an' lookin' lost. I tore off a piece of my hamburger an' held it out an' he came right over to me. I picked him up an' put him in my buddy's truck. I saw the tag on his collar, so I called this number."

Oh, my God! Oh, my God! Meghan's heart was racing. "Hold on a moment, please." Covering her hand over the phone, she let out a joyous shriek. "Everyone! Smokey's been found! He's safe!"

The dining room rang with whoops and hollers. Valerie grabbed the phone and had the young man repeat what he had told Meghan. She then asked, "Where are you?"

"Jonesboro."

"Jonesboro? But that's more than a hundred miles away from here." Her joy was instantly swamped by suspicion. Her good-for-nothing ex-husband, Dean, grew up in Jonesboro. *I wouldn't put it past him if he had a friend call and make the whole thing up just to annoy me.* "Is this some kind of crank call?" she said in an icy tone. "Did Dean put you up to this?"

"I don't know no Dean, ma'am, an' this ain't no joke. I'm in my buddy's pickup, usin' his cell phone, an' holdin' a friendly black cat wearin' a tag that has your phone number on it. He's eaten most of my burger, he's purrin', an' he seems healthy, 'cept he's pretty skinny. It's the gospel truth. Here, I'll read you the vaccination tag number, 9659JD7."

Valerie scribbled it down, opened a kitchen desk drawer, pulled out the folder marked "cats," and checked. Sure enough, it was Smokey's vaccination number.

"You *do* have Smokey!" she said, giddy with relief. "I'm sorry to have questioned you. We can be there in about two hours. I know it's Christmas Eve, but can you wait up until we arrive?"

"Yeah, sure. I haven't been 'round cats much. What do I do with him?"

"Just love him . . . and he'll love you back."

After getting directions, Valerie hung up. The girls, who had dashed off to listen to the conversation on other extensions, sprinted into the kitchen and joined their mother in a group celebratory dance. Leaving Peepaw behind, they piled into the car and drove to Jonesboro.

When they arrived at the address, which was a dilapidated mobile home in a rundown trailer park, they hesitated before knocking on the door. A lanky young man with a buzz cut and clad in grease-stained overalls answered and let them inside. He introduced them to his very pregnant wife, who was holding Smokey.

As soon as the cat saw his human family, he let out a yowl and leaped into Valerie's arms. His purr sounded like a motorboat as Meghan and Erin petted and kissed him.

"We are so incredibly grateful that you rescued our cat," Valerie said.

"I'm glad I was the one who found him, ma'am," he replied. "I gave him some water, 'cause we're out of milk. He's a friendly little feller."

While Valerie and the young man talked, the girls glanced around the trailer. Living in an upscale development, they had never seen poverty like this: a threadbare couch, a wooden chair with a duct-taped seat, a torn card table in the kitchen, lamps without shades. Taped to one wall were pages of copy paper with holiday scenes drawn with a marking pen. In the corner was a scraggly, three-foot-tall Christmas tree with a few ornaments made of paper, yarn, and aluminum foil hanging from its droopy branches. There were no presents under the tree.

Reaching into her purse for her wallet, Valerie said, "Please, let me give you a reward for saving Smokey."

He waved off the offer. "No, ma'am, I couldn't accept any money. My daddy always said that helpin' others was reward enough. I'm not sure he was includin' animals, but I think it applies."

"Okay, then, at least let us give you a tin of homemade Christmas cookies. Surely you could accept that. I'll go get it."

Knowing they had eaten all the cookies on the ride to Jonesboro, Erin said, "But, Mom, we don't —" She said no more after her mother glared at her.

As they walked back to the car, Erin whispered, "There are no cookies left, Mom."

"I know," Valerie whispered back. "Hand me the tin in the back, please."

Valerie then slipped five twenty-dollar bills into the tin container and snapped the lid shut.

"Wait, Mom," said Meghan, opening it back up. She reached into her little purse and pulled out $13, her leftover Christmas shopping money, and put it in the tin. Erin emptied her purse of $6.34 as her contribution.

"Thank you, girls," said Valerie. Turning to Meghan, she said, "Give this to them, say 'Merry Christmas,' and run back to the car. We'll be out of here before they open the tin." The plan worked perfectly.

Before dozing off during the long ride home, Erin said, "This is turning into a wonderful Christmas!"

The next morning, Smokey was his frisky old self, diving into discarded gift wrapping, jumping in and out of empty boxes, and hiding ribbons and bows throughout the house. Meanwhile, the McClearys were still wondering where their cat had been over the previous three weeks and how he had gotten so far away. It seemed the only one who knew was Smokey — and he wasn't talking.

Later that day, as the girls were taking down the flyers, they were stopped by Mrs. Appleton, who lived down the street. "Did you find your cat or have you given up?" she asked. The girls told her about Smokey's adventure. When they finished, Mrs. Appleton said, "Oh, mercy me! I know how he ended up in Jonesboro!"

The girls stared at each other for a second and then in unison said, "How?"

"About three weeks ago, my cousin from Kansas City stopped here in her RV on her way to Florida for the winter. Well, she called today to wish me a merry Christmas. She said that after they left here, they thought they heard a meow, but couldn't figure out where it was coming from. They stopped in Jonesboro for lunch, and when they stepped out of the RV, a black cat streaked out the door and disappeared. It had to be Smokey. He probably had sneaked into the RV when it was parked in my driveway, and no one saw him do it."

"That explains everything," said Meghan.

"What a stinker!" added Erin.

The morning of New Year's Eve, Peepaw came to breakfast in a foul mood. "I don't know if someone is playing a trick on me, or I'm going daffy in my old age. Before getting in the shower last night, I took out my dentures and placed them on the bathroom sink. I meant to put them in the container, but I didn't, and I was so tired after my shower, I went to sleep. This morning, I went to put my teeth back in, but they were missing. I can't find them anywhere."

Valerie and the girls searched his bathroom and bedroom and other places around the house without any luck.

"You don't think Smokey took them, do you?" Meghan asked her grandfather.

"He's definitely the prime suspect," Peepaw replied.

❋ ❋ ❋

Watching TV that evening, as the McClearys were waiting for the giant crystal ball to drop in New York City's Times Square, Peepaw had fallen asleep in his easy chair. The girls giggled because he was snoring with his toothless mouth wide open. When Valerie nudged him awake, he sputtered and mumbled something that no one could understand.

On New Year's Day, the McClearys took down all the Christmas decorations. The last to go was the tree. While Peepaw and Valerie lifted it, the girls lay on the floor, holding the tree stand so it wouldn't tip over and spill the water. Suddenly, the girls squealed with laughter.

"Peepaw, we solved the case of the missing teeth," Meghan announced.

There, in the stand's pine-needled water, were his choppers.

"We all know who put them there, don't we?" said Erin.

All eyes turned to Smokey, who was lounging on Peepaw's chair, preening himself.

Fishing the dentures out of the water, Peepaw said with a smile, "Y'all should have left him in Jonesboro."

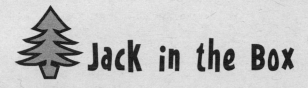# Jack in the Box

Chanise Cole sat on the edge of the couch as she watched her oldest granddaughter, eight-year-old Keesha, unwrap her last Christmas present, a stuffed rabbit. Chanise's two other grandchildren, who had come from her native Ohio to her new home in Alabama, had already ripped open all their gifts. Surveying the mound of crumpled wrapping paper and games, clothes, toys, and dolls scattered across her living room floor, Chanise said, "Santa Claus was mighty generous to all of you."

The kids and their parents nodded in agreement.

"I got everything I wanted, Gramma Chanise," declared Keesha.

"Are you sure?" questioned Chanise.

Keesha scrunched her nose and confessed, "Well, I was hoping Santa would give me a real rabbit instead of this stuffed one."

"Hmmm," said Chanise, squinting her eyes. "Is that a note wrapped around your stuffed rabbit's collar?"

Keesha unfurled the note and read it out loud, "Santa has one more gift for you by the back door."

As the girl dashed across the living room and through the kitchen, Chanise shouted, "For heaven's sake, child, wait for the rest of us." When everybody had gathered by the back door, Keesha opened it and screamed in delight. In a cage on the stoop was the most adorable rabbit she had ever seen. He had plush chestnut-colored fur and perky ears that were tipped in dark brown. His dark eyes were encircled in the same creamy white fur that covered his belly and outlined his jowls.

"I can't believe it!" Keesha squealed. "Santa got me a real, live bunny rabbit!"

With Chanise's help, the girl pulled out the rabbit and petted him. "Ooooh, he feels so velvety!" said Keesha. "Isn't he the cutest thing?"

She set the rabbit down, and he began hopping around the yard. "I know what we can call him," said Keesha. "Hopscotch!"

When the excitement died down and Hopscotch was put back in his cage, Chanise gathered the grandchildren around her and said, "I want to tell you a true story about my first rabbit, Jack in the Box. When I was Keesha's age, I wanted a pet rabbit for Christmas real bad. But I was very sick, and we were very poor. Back then, my brother, Terrell — your great-uncle, the airline pilot — and my mama, who is your great-grandma Lena, lived in what was called the projects. The projects were a group of big, ugly apartment buildings for poor people in a bad part of town. So the chances of getting my Christmas wish were slim. But I got the surprise of my life thanks to Terrell and a nice teenage boy, his daddy, and their dog. It happened a few days before Christmas Day 1965. . . ."

❄ ❄ ❄

Dan had just carried another box of toys from his dad's station wagon through the back door of the community center when a boy about ten years old walked in behind him. Snow was clinging to the boy's wiry black hair and the shoulders of his oversized jacket. His ill-fitting pants exposed the white socks between his tattered cuffs and his worn Converse All Stars. Judging from the hand-me-downs, Dan assumed the boy came from the projects.

"Is this the place where they're giving away Christmas presents?" the boy asked.

"Yes it is, but you're way too early," replied Dan. "The toy giveaway isn't scheduled to start for another ninety minutes, and we're still setting things up."

"Is it cool if I stay?"

"You're not supposed to be in here yet. People are already lining up outside. Are you registered for a toy?"

The boy looked at the floor and shook his head. "No, but I don't want anything for me. I was hoping to find something for my sister. She's real sick and —"

"No sweat. I'll get you registered so you can get a gift for her. And if you don't want to wait in line in the snow with the others, you can help me set up. Deal?"

"That's cool."

Dan held out his hand and said, "My name is Dan Masterson."

The boy hadn't had much contact with white teenagers, especially tall and skinny 15-year-olds, so he hesitated briefly before shaking Dan's hand. "I'm Terrell Larkin."

"Glad to meet you, Terrell. Help me bring in the rest of the boxes."

When the station wagon and other vehicles were unloaded, the boys assisted volunteers in sorting the presents by age group on a line of long tables that stretched from one end of the community center to the other. After they had completed the task, Dan took Terrell over to a corner where a yellow Labrador retriever with a snout white from age was curled up.

"Is this your dog?" Terrell asked.

"Yep. Meet Jessie." The dog sat up and held out her right front paw. "Go ahead. She wants to shake hands with you."

Terrell flashed a grin, revealing a missing upper tooth. He shook her paw and petted her.

"She can never get too much affection," said Dan. "I've had her since I was in kindergarten. She was a Christmas present. My parents arranged to have my uncle pick her up from the breeders when she was a puppy. He put her in a basket and then rang the doorbell and ran off. When I opened the door, there was Jessie looking up at me, wagging her tail. What a surprise. I played with her all day, but then we had to return her to the breeder because Jessie still needed her mother. She became a permanent member of our family about a month later, and she has been a great dog ever since. She turned ten two months ago. Do you have a pet?"

"No. We had a dog once, but when my dad split, he took the dog with him. That was two years ago, and we haven't seen either one since."

"What a bummer."

"That's life." Terrell shrugged. "Um, you're not giving away any real animals, are you?"

"Nope. Just stuffed ones."

After the volunteers had put out more than 300 gifts, the doors were opened and the community center filled rapidly. As children lined up for the noon giveaway, they sipped on hot chocolate and munched Christmas cookies. Each registered child was allowed to choose one present.

"Well, we're about ready to give away the toys," Dan told Terrell. "Every child has to be accompanied by an adult. I don't think you came with one."

"Mom is home taking care of my sister."

Dan introduced his father, Frank, to Terrell and explained the situation. Mr. Masterson agreed to act as the sponsoring adult for the boy and led Terrell toward the front of the line. "I don't want anything for myself," Terrell told him. "I just want to get something for my sister, Chanise. She's sick and has to go to the hospital for blood transfusions on a regular basis and has missed a lot of school. She's in third grade, one year behind me."

Terrell looked at the toys in Chanise's age group and zeroed in on the table loaded with stuffed animals. He sifted through them until he found a white plush rabbit. "I think she'll really like this one," he said.

Mr. Masterson said, "Pick out something for yourself, Terrell."

"But I thought it was only one present for each kid."

"It is. But you got something for your sister who can't be here, so it's only fair you get a gift, too."

"Cool, thanks!" Terrell studied the table for his age group and selected a model airplane. "I want to be a pilot when I grow up," he said.

The toy giveaway was a huge success. After the happy crowd had filtered out, Dan began cleaning up when he spotted Terrell in the corner with Jessie. The teen walked over and said, "Are you waiting for someone to pick you up?"

"No. I walked here."

"Where do you live?"

"In the projects on Eighth Street."

"But that's on the other side of the city. Man, that's a long way to walk, especially in the snow. The community center on Ninth Street held a toy giveaway yesterday near your home. Why didn't you go there?"

"I did. I wanted to get a stuffed rabbit for Chanise, but by the time I got to choose, they were all gone. So I thought I'd try the giveaway here for the kids from the Washington Avenue projects." Clutching the stuffed rabbit, he asked, "I can still keep it, can't I?"

"Of course. My dad and I will drive you home after this place is cleaned up. Meanwhile, I'm going to take Jessie for a walk. Want to come with me?"

"Cool."

About four inches of snow had fallen, turning the otherwise drab inner-city landscape into a cheerier setting. At least for a little while, the snow covered the neighborhood's litter as the trio walked past abandoned buildings, barred windows, and graffiti on the walls.

With the temperatures remaining in the twenties, the snow had yet to melt, even though the sun was peeking out now and then from behind rolling gray clouds. Jessie frolicked in the snow, sticking her nose in it and playfully trying to bite the snowballs the boys tossed at her. Because it wasn't a wet snow, the snowballs were powdery, so when she chomped on them, they burst into white poofs.

"She might be old, but she still has the spirit of a puppy," said Dan.

"It'd be cool to have a pet again. Chanise asked Santa for a real one, but she'll have to settle for a stuffed bunny."

"Won't your mom let her have a rabbit?"

Terrell shrugged. "Chanise sort of had a rabbit that she played with. His name was Domino, because he was black and white. He belonged to Griz — a loser who lives down the hall with his dumb girlfriend, Sheila. They kept Domino in their apartment for a while. But then Griz decided that he didn't like Domino all that much, because the rabbit didn't always use his litter box and was kind of messy. So they kept him in a cage in the basement.

"Chanise would go down there and play with Domino. He was really friendly. Then one day, she went down there, and Domino was gone. We looked everywhere, so I knocked on Griz's door and asked him what happened to the rabbit. Griz said that it wasn't fair to the rabbit to keep him in the basement all the time, so they got rid of him.

"When I asked where he was, Sheila and Griz nearly split a gut. They said they put Domino in the car and went to the pet store. When they were in the parking lot, they stuffed him into a big purse. Then they walked into the store and went to where the rabbits were kept. Griz thought it was funny that Domino was thumping around in Sheila's purse. They waited until no one was looking, and they opened an empty cage and shoved Domino inside it and latched the door. Then they booked it out of there.

"When Griz was telling me how he dumped Domino, Sheila was laughing the whole time. That really frosted me. Griz said it was a win for everyone. He told me, 'We got rid of the rabbit, the pet store got to sell him twice, and he got a new home.'"

"Why didn't he just give Domino to your sister?" Dan asked.

"Griz is bad news. And Sheila is no better. They're the pits. They knew how much Chanise loved that rabbit. Yeah, she's been sick, but she would've taken good care of him. And if she couldn't, I would have until she got well."

During the boys' walk, the clouds thickened and the wind picked up. "Looks like it's going to snow again," said Dan. "Let's head back to the center. Then we'll drive you home."

After they turned around, Dan noticed that Jessie wasn't following them. The dog had kept walking in the opposite direction toward a large trash bin in the alley about 50 feet away. "Jessie, come here, girl!" Dan shouted.

But the dog, with her nose in the snow and her ears alert, ignored his command and kept sniffing around the trash bin.

"Jessie!"

The dog turned her head, looked at Dan, and whimpered. Then she stood on her hind legs, put her front paws on the bin, and began barking in a high-pitched tone.

"She wants us to come over there," said Dan. "I wonder what she's found."

After hurrying to her side, Dan said, "What is it, girl?"

Jessie barked and pawed at the side of the trash bin, so Dan hoisted himself and looked inside it. "I don't see anything but frozen garbage and trash bags and boxes," he told Terrell. Just as Dan was about to lower himself, a small cardboard box wrapped in duct tape shook ever so slightly. "That's weird."

"What's weird?" asked Terrell.

"I don't know if my mind is playing tricks on me or if I actually saw a box move." He stared at it for several seconds until it jiggled again. "I think there's something in the box — something alive!"

While Jessie continued to bark, Dan leaped into the bin and picked up the box. He leaned over the side, handed it to Terrell, and jumped out. As soon as Terrell set the box on the snow-covered ground, Jessie circled it, barking and wagging her tail in excitement.

Dan pulled out his Boy Scout pocketknife and carefully sliced open the top. To the boys' and Jessie's surprise, out popped a steel-gray rabbit! With its big ears flattened against its back in a sign of fear, the animal took one look at the boys and the dog and tried to scamper away. But Jessie quickly cornered it without harming it.

"Holy smokes! The rabbit came out of there like a Jack in the Box," Dan declared.

Terrell scooped up the trembling rabbit and gently stroked its head between its ears. "There, there, you'll be all right," he said in a soothing voice.

Jessie kept jumping around Terrell, wanting to sniff the rabbit and get a better look at it until Dan called her off and had her sit still.

"What sort of heartless person would seal a rabbit in a box and toss it in the trash bin on a freezing cold day?" Dan muttered.

"In this neighborhood? There are plenty who would."

"Obviously the culprit no longer wanted it."

"At least Griz returned his rabbit to the store . . . and he's a scuzzball. The creep who did this to the rabbit is a psycho."

Dan suggested, "Maybe we should call the police."

Terrell scoffed at the thought. "The cops won't do anything. With all the crime that happens here, do you really think they have time to go after someone who doesn't like rabbits?"

"You're right," said Dan. "There aren't a whole lot of clues, anyway. The only footprints around the trash bin are ours. That means the culprit threw the box in the bin before the snowfall. That rabbit is lucky to be alive."

"It would have died in there if it hadn't been for your dog," said Terrell.

Dan bent over and rubbed his dog's face. "You saved a life, Jessie! Good girl!"

As they headed back to the center, Terrell cradled the rabbit in his arms. Sensing it was safe, the animal stopped trembling. Jessie pranced beside the boys, obviously pleased she had done something good.

Noticing that Terrell was lost in thought and grinning, Dan told him, "I know exactly what you're going to do with that rabbit."

"Yeah, maybe you can give the stuffed bunny that I had picked out for Chanise to someone else."

At the center, Dan found a leftover red bow and attached it to the real rabbit's neck. On the way to taking Terrell home, Dan and his dad stopped at a pet store and bought a cage and other supplies. When they arrived at the projects, they had to walk up the stairs to his fourth-floor apartment because the elevator, as usual, wasn't working.

Before they reached the door to his apartment, Terrell told Dan and his father, "Thanks for everything. And thanks, Dan, for giving me the idea of what to name the rabbit. This is going to be a Christmas that Chanise will never forget."

While her grandchildren sat quietly at her feet, Chanise wrapped up her story. "When Terrell came in with Jack in the Box, I screamed just like Keesha did today," Chanise recalled. "Oh, I put a lovin' on that bunny for more than seven years, and he loved me back. He was my best friend. He liked to cuddle with me and brought me great comfort when I was sick and helped get me well again. Yes, that was a Christmas I'll never forget."

"Gramma Chanise," said Keesha, "this is a Christmas I'll never forget, either!"

The Christmas Day Wonder

Through sleepy eyes, Sarah gazed out her kitchen window and sighed. "Oh dear, not again," she muttered to herself. Last night's snow lay in foot-deep marshmallow drifts. To most people, the snow was beautiful and couldn't have come at a better time. After all, it was Christmas morning. What could be better? But to Sarah, the snow represented a harsh reality. Now she would have to get out in the cold and clear off the front steps and cement sidewalk, a task she had done three days earlier after the last snowfall.

Just because today was Christmas did nothing to lighten the elderly woman's mood. In her mind, today was merely one more bleak and lonely winter day in the farm country of north-central Pennsylvania. No decorated Christmas tree posed in the front window. No gaily wrapped presents were stacked underneath. No lights twinkled a cheery greeting.

It wasn't always that way. Her brick ranch house used to throb with the laughter and glee of children ripping open their gifts from Santa. But today it was silent — a stark reminder of life before her son, Ben, and daughter, Beth, grew up and moved away and before her beloved husband died. Although Sarah had been a widow for many years, not a single day went by that she didn't miss him. Christmas without him only made her heart ache more.

Her frame of mind brightened a bit when she thought about Beth. *She'll probably call this afternoon,* Sarah thought. *It'll be nice to hear her voice and catch up on her busy life. It was so sweet of her to send me such a nice check. I'll put the money to good use.*

Ben was in the Navy far from home. She had no idea if or when he would be able to call her. *Maybe he'll surprise me, and I'll hear from him today. But I better not get my hopes up.*

Being alone was difficult at times, especially during the holidays. Other than Beth's phone call, there was no reason to expect today would be different from any other.

Because of her arthritis and her age — she was 69 — Sarah was not as steady on her feet as she once was. Every winter she worried about slipping and falling on ice. She tried to be careful and always made sure to sprinkle salt on her front steps to melt any ice and snow. Only when the steps were clear would she venture farther outside and take care of the sidewalk. It was too hard for her to shovel snow, so she would use a sturdy broom to sweep it away and create a narrow path to her mailbox.

Maybe I should wait a few days until it warms up before I try to clear off the snow, she thought. *There's no mail delivery today, so why bother? But on the other hand, if it snows again tonight, it might get too deep for me to deal with. I better take care of it now, just to be on the safe side.*

Dressed in a nightgown and heavy bathrobe, Sarah pulled on her boots and winced. The stiffness and discomfort from her arthritis made even this simple act difficult. Occasionally, the pain seemed more than she could tolerate, but on this morning it was the ache of loneliness that caused her the most distress.

Grasping a small salt-filled can, Sarah opened the front door and tossed salt on the snow-covered, icy steps. Within seconds she heard the familiar faint crackle that indicated the salt was beginning to change the ice and snow to slush.

Gingerly she eased her way outside. Reaching into the can for another handful of salt, Sarah suddenly lost her balance and fell. Down she tumbled, hitting the steps hard, until she wound up flat on her back on the sidewalk.

Having the breath knocked out of her, she lay stunned by the impact. After a moment, she attempted to get up, but the effort caused such pain that she cried out in agony and lay back down. She tried a few more times. But with the slightest movement, stabbing pain radiated from her back and down her legs.

Oh, dear Lord, I can't get up and I can't even crawl back into the house. I can't do anything! Sarah began sobbing, more from alarm than the hurt.

She discovered that if she lay absolutely still, the pain was tolerable. Her mind had been so focused on her dilemma that she hadn't thought much about the temperature, which was in the low thirties. But now she was beginning to shiver. *I wish I had put on my winter coat.* She clutched the bathrobe tighter around her neck, hoping to ward off the penetrating chill. Unfortunately, that did little to stop her slender body from shaking. The only way to get warmed up was to get back in the house — an impossible task for the injured woman.

Just a few feet away, her front door remained slightly open, beckoning her to safety and warmth. How close it was made no difference. It was still out of her reach.

Is this how I am going to die? By freezing to death? And on this day, of all days? She had no neighbors nearby and wasn't expecting anyone to drop by today. Still, fear compelled her to call out, "Help me! Please, someone, help me!" She yelled until her body grew too weak and her voice grew too hoarse to continue.

She began to surrender to the bitter cold. Hypothermia — the loss of body heat — was luring her into a potentially deadly sleep. *I'm so tired, so very, very tired. I'll just let go and drift off. After I sleep for a while, I'll wake up and try yelling again for help. I'm so tired.* She fell into a deep slumber as her body temperature began to drop.

Later, not knowing how much time had passed, Sarah

stirred slightly, enough to think, *I wish that annoying bug would go away.* Still in a fog, she brushed her face with her hand, trying to get rid of the bug. But it wouldn't leave. It kept bothering her. *I just want to sleep.*

Pestered by the bug, Sarah gradually woke up. Her mind needed a few seconds to process what she was now seeing through her fluttering eyes. It was no aggravating bug that had awakened her. It was the wet tongue of a scruffy-looking dog, a light brown collie mix.

Startled, Sarah tried to move away, but the searing pain reminded her that she couldn't. When the dog realized she was awake, his white-tipped tail started wagging vigorously. Then, with a big sigh, he lay down right on top of Sarah's chest. At first, his 30-pound weight made her want to shove him off, but she didn't because she felt the warmth of his body bringing life back into her.

He probably heard me calling for help. But where in the world did he come from? I've never seen him before. I wonder whose dog he is. "Hello, boy," she said, gently stroking his long-haired coat. "I'm sure glad you showed up." The dog looked at her with his big brown eyes and panted. "You are so sweet. Do you have a name?"

Sarah looked at the tag that dangled from his collar and gasped in amazement. Her body quivered when she discovered that this loving animal that came out of nowhere to give her comfort shared the exact same name as her late husband. "Barney, what a strange and wonderful coincidence," she told the dog while rubbing the white blaze on his nose. "Barney was always there for me . . . and now you, Barney the dog, are here for me." She gave him a hug.

From the looks of him, the dog hadn't received much tender loving care recently. He was thin and had a tangled coat matted with dirt. But to Sarah, he was beautiful. "Please don't leave me, Barney," she said. He didn't, remaining draped over her as another slow hour passed.

"What a good, brave dog you are," she told him. "My front door is open, and you could simply walk inside to a warm house. Yet you've chosen to stay with me. I never knew a dog could be so caring."

Having him on top of her not only kept her warm, but also awake and hopeful. To pass the time, she talked to him about her life, her children, and how much she still missed her husband. While Sarah talked, Barney occasionally whined or barked as if he understood everything she was saying.

Eventually, Sarah felt fatigued and numb from the cold except for her chest, which Barney continued to cover with his body. "Barney, I don't know how much longer I can last. I'm getting weaker and —" She stopped when she heard the telephone ring in her house. "Oh dear, that must be

Beth." *If only I could get to the phone. But I can't. I wonder, could Barney? It's absurd to think he could understand, much less actually follow, my instructions. But he's my only hope.*

"Barney, go get the phone," she asked softly, trying to mask the urgency in her voice, because she didn't want to spook him.

The dog cocked his head and stared at her, unsure what she meant.

Pointing toward the door, Sarah repeated, "Barney, please, get the phone."

His ears twitched and he turned his head toward the door. But he didn't move. Sarah pleaded with him once again to get the phone, which was on the coffee table in the living room. *Oh, what a silly woman I am,* she told herself. *It's foolish to believe this dog understands me. And what's he going to do if he did* follow my command? He can't talk. But there was something about Barney that made her believe he did understand.

Finally, the dog rose, took two steps toward the door, and then turned around and looked at her, as if wanting reassurance he was doing the right thing. For the last time, Sarah begged Barney to get the phone.

Her heart pounded with hope when the dog trotted into the house and out of sight. She heard the phone ring one more time. Then it fell silent. *Oh no! They hung up.* Seconds later, Barney reappeared at the door.

"You tried, didn't you? Thank you, boy." Sarah allowed herself to feel disappointed even though she thought, *I was asking him to do the impossible*. "Come here, Barney. Please, boy, come to me." The dog walked down the steps and snuggled with her. "What a wonderful dog you are," she said, holding him closer. "You could have stayed inside, but still you came back to me."

Sarah had been lying on the sidewalk for nearly four hours and knew she didn't have much longer to live, not in this cold. As the temperatures remained near freezing, hypothermia gripped Sarah, and she could feel herself losing consciousness. But each time she closed her eyes, Barney licked her face and whined. *He's trying . . . to keep . . . me alive.*

Suddenly, Barney bolted upright and stared at the dirt road in front of the house. Seconds later, Sarah heard a car. As it came closer, she tried to yell, but she didn't have the strength. *Please stop here. Please.* It did. Moments later, she looked up and, to her everlasting relief, saw a police officer.

After Sarah explained what had happened, he radioed for an ambulance and covered her in a blanket. Within minutes, emergency medical technicians arrived. As she was loaded onto the gurney, Sarah grasped the officer's hand and said, "Please look after the dog. He kept me alive."

"Don't worry, ma'am," he assured her. "I'll keep him until you return home."

Sarah was taken to the hospital, where she remained for a week, recovering from hypothermia and a severely injured disc in her spine. While there, she was buoyed by a phone call from Ben and a visit by Beth. Her daughter listened in awe as Sarah recounted Barney's heroics.

"Mom, I didn't even know you had a dog," said Beth. "I had called to wish you a merry Christmas. I let the phone ring a long time until it was finally answered. But all I heard was a strange breathing sound. I was frantic with worry and imagined that you were lying in the house, injured and unable to speak. I hung up and immediately phoned the police to check on you. It's amazing that the dog knocked the phone off the coffee table. He saved your life!"

"Except for when he went into the house to get the phone, he never left my side," said Sarah. "And, honey, there is something else you should know. I never saw that dog before in my life."

At Sarah's request, Beth talked to the officer the following day and told him, "Barney isn't my mother's dog, but she dearly wants him. So if his owner isn't found, my mom will give him a home."

When Sarah was released from the hospital, she had only one thing on her mind: Barney. That afternoon the officer brought the dog to the house. Bounding up to her, Barney danced around her, looking even prettier than she remembered. He had been well fed and bathed, and his long coat was now shiny, soft, and brushed.

Sarah thanked the officer for caring for Barney.

"My pleasure," he replied. "The good news is that the owner never claimed him, so Barney belongs to you. He's quite a Christmas gift."

"A glorious gift." Bending over to kiss the dog, Sarah said, "He's proven to be the most unselfish creature I've ever known. I love him."

Later as she sat on the couch with Barney at her feet, Sarah thought about how marvelously odd it was that the dog and her husband had the same name. Her husband had loved dogs all his life, but after he died, Sarah didn't want to take on the responsibility of caring for a pet. That is, until Christmas day when Barney the dog came into her life . . . and saved it.

Sarah would never solve the mystery surrounding the dog's origin, but that didn't matter. With Barney by her side, she would never be lonely again.

Adapted, by permission, from the true story "Barney" by Lynn Seely.

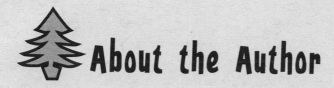 # About the Author

Allan Zullo is the author of more than 100 nonfiction books on subjects ranging from sports and the supernatural to history and animals.

He has written the bestselling Haunted Kids series, published by Scholastic, which is filled with chilling stories based on, or inspired by, documented cases from the files of ghost hunters. Allan also has introduced Scholastic readers to the Ten True Tales series, about people who have met the challenges of dangerous, sometimes life-threatening, situations. Among other books, he has authored *The Dog Who Saved Christmas and Other True Animal Tales, Miracle Pets: True Tales of Courage and Survival,* and *Bad Pets on the Loose!*

Allan, the grandfather of five and the father of two daughters, lives with his wife, Kathryn, on the side of a mountain near Asheville, North Carolina. To learn more about the author, visit his website at www.allanzullo.com.